A MIRAGE FOR MEN

LE' HANZ

HOUSE OF CAZACO
LIBERATE LEONEL

Published by HOC Publishing
houseofcazacollc@gmail.com
Copyright ©
2025 by Le' Hanz

*To all those past and present who never lost faith in their fight
against the system of injustice.*

AUTHOR'S WORDS

As a man, I've learned that one cannot make excuses for our actions once we become aware.

I've made mistakes in my life due to youthfulness, ignorance, impulsiveness, immaturity, lack of proper guidance, bad influences from my surroundings, and not having a parental figure in my life during crucial development stages.

I've lived on the streets since the tender age of nine. A man-child having to figure out everything on my own. The only thing I thought about was staying alive and figuring out how to get my next meal.

How many other children have suffered the same fate silently, thinking that the abuse and neglect they've endured is normal? To experience things of that nature is enough to traumatize a child, leaving deep physical and emotional wounds that, even when healed, leave permanent scars.

ACKNOWLEDGMENTS

There's a conviction called the 3 "F's" that I live by, and it is one of the few things that motivates and pushes me in the direction that I now find myself, after years of trying to find my way and do what I know is righteous. Never in life did I think I would write anything but a letter to my family and loved ones. I love reading books, but becoming a writer was something I never considered. Now that I have completed my first book and learned the nuances, it has become an acquired taste for me.

The three F's is a bedrock foundation for me.

Freedom is what motivates me. The ability to do what you want in the way that you want without being constrained or shackled to an ideology. The freedom to live, the freedom to love, and the freedom to place value on things that are important to you.

Family is the key to life and all that it entails. It is the crucial pillar that we build on that sets one apart from others. Family is the bond that holds us together and supports our efforts no matter the cost or time it takes to build what will ultimately be our legacy.

Emmee, Aiden, Janet, Alfreda, Dominique, Rosalie, Nardine, Frantz, Dorothy; thank you all for the support and sacrifices.

A true and genuine friend is valuable because of its rarity, as it is hard to come by. A person that is for you without any strings attached, who seeks nothing in return nor is motivated by self-interest. One who can relate to you, and is understanding and patient in their friendship. I am lucky to have found some who fit that bill. Ones I consider genuine.

Janet, Lou Sims, Unique, Smooth, Rob "E", Jim, Sp, Big Baby, Lazarus, Big Bull, Spoogie and several others; thank you all for your friendship. You are all worthy.

To Geraldine Nisbett, I owe you everything. You dedicated your life to raising me into a man and making me feel at home in a big family that had so many personalities. You taught me how to survive. My life and yours are entwined, and I miss you.

To Janet Cazaco, thank you for pushing me to be the best version of myself and not what others want me to be. For believing in me when others didn't, for placing herself on the battlefield ready to fight those she deemed our foes, for her deep and unrestrained love that I could never do without, and for the wisdom she possesses that is far beyond her years, which has made me wiser by teaching me the dangers of getting on a loving woman's bad side.

To Nardine and David, for the support and love that you gave me during the worst times, and for traveling from another country to see me although it was costly. You made sure that I felt loved from a distance because you thought I was deserving of it. I appreciate it all.

To Alfreda Cazako, who decades ago planted the seed of becoming an author in my mind, for insistently pressing me to write my story for years, although she didn't know what that story was or the depth of the tragic events that shaped me as a man. A woman who took it upon herself to acknowledge my existence in a world that shuns people, and stereotypes black men as problematic and violent, although we are an endangered species. Thanks for the love and support.

To Dom and Rosalie, for embracing me from the very beginning and accepting me even though my situation was precarious at best, and for loving me and fighting for me in your own silent way. Dominique, although it took you longer, you finally came around, but I understand that it takes time to get where we are now.

Of course Aiden, you are meant to be so much. Just stay focused and you will come into yourself in time. I expect you to be a great man.

Emmee my lil-lion, I will hear your roar and I will make sure that you are guided in the direction that will guarantee you the best success. I love you champ. Thanks for making me a proud father.

Leonel Cazaco

A MIRAGE FOR MEN

PROLOGUE

DAMN.

Today was the day. I couldn't believe it was time for my fate to be decided. Some stranger, some random man who knew nothing about my life, my struggles, my pain, was going to decide my fate.

I sat on a hard metal bench in the bullpen of the federal court building on Broad Street in Richmond, Virginia, was everything that had led to this moment. I was in a Maryland county jail for a while, serving time for a probation violation from 1989, and just got transferred from MCIJ in Jessup, Maryland. Stupidity got the best of me, putting me in a nonsensical situation where I was pulled over on I-95 with cocaine in my car and arrested.

Now here I was in 1997, sitting in another courthouse, awaiting another sentencing. The only difference here was that I would be against a hard-liner Bush-appointed judge in federal court. And if that wasn't enough, I faced a lifetime sentence for alleged RICO violations. I beat the worst charges they threw at me, but there were still many hurdles to overcome.

Yet somehow I still held onto a hint of optimism as I got up from the bench, trying to break free from negative thoughts. They never proved anything solid about me, just a bunch of BS witness statements from people looking to get better deals on their own cases. I had bigger stuff to think about. But no matter how hard I tried, reality sunk in right then.

I was alone for my sentencing. All of the other defendants in the case were to be sentenced separately, even though the court tried us jointly. There was little else I could do but pace back and forth, trying to rationalize.

I should be alright, I thought. *If I get 20 years, I'll be 40 at the most when I get out. That's doable. I can handle that.*

I felt a tad bit better, though I hoped the time I served would be less.

I was acquitted of all murders attributed to me by a jury of my so-called "peers." A co-defendant exonerated me from what I was convicted of, but since his statement was given during own sentencing and not at trial, I couldn't reap any of its benefits.

I stopped pacing as a US Marshal came to the bars of my cell. "Mr. Cazaco."

"Yes," I nervously replied.

"It's time to go. I gotta put these on you."

He handcuffed my wrists and ankles, then proceeded to put a belt--connected to a black box--on me. If activated, 50,000 volts of electric charge would course through my body, and I'd be pissing and shitting myself in court. I was considered that dangerous.

They brought me into the courtroom for the proceedings to begin. The room was massive, the bench impossibly high above the chair I was seated in, and the people in the room seemed entirely different from me. I was in a daze during the beginning of the hearing. I knew eventually it would be time for my fate to be decided.

The judge, a middle aged white man, looked over the courtroom as he spoke, addressing my two attorneys first. "Mr. Barley, Mr. Bowen, I don't know whether you're aware of it or not, but during his sentencing, Mr. Thomas proffered to the court, by his lawyer, that during the murders, Mr. Cazaco fired no shots. That was brought to the attention of the court just before...I really don't know whether counsel for Mr. Cazaco was even in the room at the time."

"We were, your honor," My lawyer responded. "Could you reiterate, for the record, what our client's co-defendant said."

That eased my nerves, allowing me to breathe a little easier by the time I was given an opportunity to speak on my own behalf.

"The government knows I didn't kill nobody," I said. "Leonel Cazaco did not order no hit at the murder location, there wasn't even testimony to that. As for selling drugs, I cannot refute that. I sold a lot of them, but not in or with no organization that the government mentioned. I got sentenced to 20 years for my actions in regards to that already, and without my pleading guilty to those counts, you wouldn't have been able to convict me on that, cause it was the same cocaine that the indictment alleges, so I feel like I am being punished twice for the same acts. If you're going to punish me, punish me for something I did, not something people allege I did. That's all."

That took a lot out of me, but I felt better having said it. I made myself heard to the jurors and judge. I stood up for myself against the government.

"Alright, Mr. Cazaco, you may stand up."

It was time.

My lawyers and I rose.

This was it. The moment of truth was here.

"The record is clear that there is ample evidence to support each of the convictions and the participation of Mr. Cazaco as an active participant in the murders for which he's been convicted, and he was otherwise convicted by ample evidence of complicity in each of the crimes for which he was in fact convicted."

My heart was sinking as the judge made his statement.

"He was shown mercy by the jury in deliberations respective to those duties. I will therefore now pass judgement and render my sentence."

My heart was beating a mile a minute.

"Pursuant to the Sentencing Reform Act of 1984, it is the judgement of this court that the defendant, Leonel R. Cazaco, is hereby committed to the custody of the United States Bureau of Prisons for the term of life, plus 300 months."

The world went silent for me at that very moment. My entire life, from childhood until this very moment, flashed before my eyes. My senses numbed and blocked out everything. Whatever was said sounded like an incomprehensible guttural language in my ears.

All I was focused on, all I could comprehend, was that I did not deserve the sentence that I got.

"The most powerful defense is to never present yourself as a target."

1

———

FLIGHT

IT'S 4:30 AM.

My grandmother, Geraldine Nisbett, was awake by now, getting ready for work. She always made breakfast and came in to check on me before leaving. I cherished Mama. For many years of my life, I believed she was my mother, because she taught me everything I knew. On this particular morning, I had no idea how close I was to learning the truth.

I heard her quiet footsteps approaching my bed and woke up, looking around the dark room while doing my best to act like I was asleep. Mama knew better.

"Mi nuh yuh sleep, Leonel," she whispered.

I turned over, trying not to wake my aunt, who was fast asleep next to me.

"I'm up," I said. Then, with a level of excitement only little kids can muster, I scrunched up my face and prepared to ask her the same question I did every morning. It was part of the ritual.

"Can I go with you?"

I was prepared, and completely ready, for the standard

answer. The answer she gave me every time. The answer that was part of the ritual: a kind and loving, but firm *"No!"*

This time, she smiled, leaned down, kissed me on the forehead and said, "Hurry and get dressed. Meet me in the front yard."

No longer caring if I woke my aunt, I jumped out of the bed. It didn't matter if I had woken the whole world. My grandmother said yes! She was going to let me come with her to the market. I was dressed and outside in minutes, not bothering with breakfast. Mama would take care of me. I was her first grandson, and she adored me.

WE ARRIVED AT THE MARKET. It was large and sprawling. People from all over would come to buy household things, food, anything and everything you could imagine. It seemed like it would take years and years to catalogue all that was sold there. I enjoyed going with Mama because she always spoiled me. I would get everything I liked in one day: sugarcane, mango, jellied coconut. We had even stopped to eat some fried dumplings with fried fish, and Mama bought me sorrel juice.

After an hour of walking around, I was stuffed. I can't remember a time outside of the market that I ever ate so much, or so well.

At some point, I spotted my friend Ozzie, who lived two houses down from me. I walked over to him, and we both grinned at each other, then walked ahead talking, getting each other caught up on things around our neighborhood. Far ahead of everyone else, we stopped to grab a drink and waited. It wasn't long before I saw my grandmother with three bags in her hands, ready to head home.

IT WAS 1:00 in the afternoon by the time we were back at the house, and everyone was awake.

My uncle was there. He was Rastafarian and I loved it when he visited. I learned a lot from him, mostly about the Bible, and made sure to listen intently when he spoke. Not so much out of interest, but because I was waiting for him to light the spliff I knew he had.

Mama always chased him out of the house, but that was well after we smoked. By then, I was ready for him to go. I grew tired of hearing him drone on about the Rasta shit.

Laid on my bed, hungry from the weed, I waited for Mama to cook. I didn't know how drowsy I was until I fell into a deep, deep sleep, not even waking up for dinner. Unaware that this was to be my last night in the house with Mama.

SOMEONE WAS SHAKING ME.

As my brain jolted awake in the early hours of the morning, I realized it was Mama. I was dumbstruck. This was not part of the morning routine.

I didn't hear her quiet footsteps. I didn't wake up so she could chastise me and say she knew I wasn't sleeping. I didn't have a chance to ask her if I could go with her to the market.

Everything was different.

"Wake up, wake up," Mama said. "Someone is here to see you."

Even at seven years old, I heard the urgency in Mama's voice. I knew it must be important. Mama would have let me sleep if it was just one of my friends. And living with her afforded me the ability to sleep in as late as I wanted before I had to get up and do chores.

Mama led me into the living room where a stranger with a smile on her face was standing. I'd never seen this woman before. But I knew she must be important by how she looked at me.

Mama pushed me toward her. "Go ahead," she said, "that's your mother."

"My mother?" I asked.

Mama nodded.

Wasn't Mama my mother? I thought.

I couldn't comprehend what this all meant. How could this other woman be my mother too? But if Mama was telling me this, I knew that it must have been true.

"Come here, Leonel," the stranger said. "I'm Merlene, your mother. I'm taking you with me. Go get your things. We have a plane to catch."

I ran away from her, trying to hide myself.

Mama had raised me. She was the strongest woman I knew and the only woman I've known as my mother. I didn't know this other woman at all. Why should I go with her? Who was she to me?

Mama came to me with tears in her eyes as she recognized the tantrum that was building.

"I don't wanna go with her!" I yelled.

"She's your mother," Mama said.

"I don't even know her," I blubbered, crying harder than I can ever remember.

"There is nothing I can do," Mama said. "She is your mother, and she wants to take you home with her. I have no choice but to let you go. If you don't like it, maybe we can figure out how to let you come back here."

This cheered me a little.

I packed my few possessions in a bag, and left with this woman claiming to be my mother. She was no more my mother than the country she was taking me to—the United States—was my home. It was there where my new mother had been living since I was fifteen months old, after she left me in the care of Mama. I didn't know anything about the United States and I didn't know who this woman was. Despite this, both were my future.

It was a whirlwind of activity as she grabbed my bags, put them into a waiting car, and hurried me along. As the car drove off, all I could do was look out the back window, trying to see Mama and my aunts. The ride to the airport was silent. Neither of us was sure what to say to the other.

She made some attempts to start a conversation, like explaining how she left me in the care of Mama when I was fifteen months old to live in the United States, but I was indifferent. I was still trying to comprehend why this was happening to me. I thought it was my fault, but I couldn't understand what I had done to cause this. All I wanted was for this stranger, my new mother, to finally give up and send me back to Mama's house.

During the car ride, I thought about Mama: how she would wake me on Saturdays to go to church with her and listen to the preacher, who I couldn't stand. I would gladly go sit in that church for days and weeks on end if it meant returning to Mama's house. Have everything go back to how it was.

You never know how much you love someone until they are ripped from your life.

I was jolted out of my reverie by someone shaking my shoulder, bringing me back to a place where I was unhappy, disappointed, hurt, and confused. I was taken from memories-- pleasant moments filled with love--and slammed back to this new reality. A reality in which I had no control.

My new mother led the way, and before I could take two steps out of the car, I froze.

This was my first time at an airport. There was so much going on around me. It was busy like the market where Mama took me to, but to a crazier degree. All of the sensations, the noise, the people, the movement, it was all totally new to me. I hadn't even made it to the United States, yet I could already feel how this experience was affecting me. I didn't like it.

2

PARADISE LOST

I ARRIVED in the states in the early 80s and things already were not looking up. I knew from the beginning that it wasn't going to work. For starters, my new mother saw aspects of my birth father in me, and her hatred of him carried over into how she treated me. She tried not to let it affect her, but it did. I could tell from the plane ride alone.

It was snowing when we landed. I was amazed as I stared out the window, as I had never seen snow before, and sat there: a big-eyed kid watching it fall. As the plane descended, I could make out the lights of New York off in the distance. I was a young boy entering a new world. The rules were going to be different, and as far as I could tell, survival was life and death.

My new mother--at this point, just "my mother"--already had another son. So not only was I getting a new mother, but I was getting a new brother. In some kind of fairy tale, this would have signified the happy ending. In my story, this was the miserable beginning of Cinderella's story.

My mother doted on her other son, making sure everything was provided for him.

Our relationship, on the other hand, was strained from the start, and never became any less tense. I'm pretty sure that it all boils down to the fact that I could never call her "Mom." I left the only mother I knew behind, on an island that was my paradise. Even the things that I thought were struggles back home really weren't; I had family to help me through tragic moments and rough times. Sure, we may have had to survive by the labor of our own hands, but what kept us full and warm was the love we got from Mama, who made sure that our every need was met. There was not a day or night where she wasn't working hard to keep a roof over our heads and food on the table. This was a woman who had ten children and raised them all by herself.

After debarking the plane, my mother took my hand and walked us through the airport terminal. A man--her husband--waited for us outside.

My mother, I had learned, had started her life over right after she left me with Mama. She got married and had a son. As the years went by she became pregnant again. For some reason, while pregnant with her second child, she decided that she needed to snatch me back from Mama, but I never felt like I was actually part of the family.

There was never time for my mother to give me the maternal love I craved, there was never a chance for us to bond in the normal way a mother and son might. This missing piece was huge. It left a gaping hole in what might have been a tough, but ultimately meaningful relationship. I never got to find out what would have happened if we had both reconciled our differences and made an effort to mend fences and salvage our relationship. We let our anger and our hatred toward one another maintain us

For all I know, if we figured out how to love each other, perhaps it could have saved us. Maybe this love could have saved me from the streets. Saved me from rebellion. If we could have looked past our hatred of each other, perhaps everything in my life might have been different.

We got into a car with her husband, and we drove to where I was going to live. This was to be my home. At least until I'd upset them so much they would decide to send me away.

I didn't know what to make of their house when we arrived. It was an apartment complex, a stack of buildings where everyone lived side-by-side. It looked tiny from the outside.

When inside, I saw that it was much bigger than I originally thought. It was a three-and-a-half bedroom apartment with two bathrooms. The kitchen and living room were decently sized. The living room, however, was off limits.

No one, especially me, was allowed in the living room.

My mother cherished the furniture there, as well as the collection of dolls she scattered around the room. It was creepy. I'm honestly not sure I would have gone into the living room even if I could have.

She showed me my room. As she left the room, I sat down on the bed not sure of what else to do. I stared at the walls, looked around, and felt completely out of place, even though I was sitting on something referred to as "my bed."

After a few minutes, she brought in a small boy, introducing him as my "half brother." I looked at him and he looked at me, both strangers to one another. I had no idea what a "half brother" was.

What does that even mean? I thought.

He looked like a whole person.

Over the next few years, that phrase drove a wedge between him and I. Every time my mother referred to him as my "half brother" did something to our relationship. She said those words so often it was almost a mantra. I was reminded of the fact that he was my half brother at every single opportunity, especially when his father was there. I had always believed that if you had the same mother, you were just brothers or sisters. Apparently, in the United States, the relationships were far more blurry.

The school I was signed up for wasn't too far from the neighborhood we lived in. The area was nice, and there were a lot of kids around my own age. I blended in as best as I could. If it weren't for the language barrier, no one would have known I wasn't born and raised there. I spoke English well enough, but there were times when I'd slip or get upset and the raw Caribbean would come out.

I became friends with a few of the neighborhood kids like Lamont, Mark, Jack, but there were those who didn't like me because they thought I was different. My thick accent caused a lot of conflict.

Many of the neighborhood girls gave me attention because they found my accent attractive. I didn't really care about the conflict it caused. I enjoyed the attention.

Most of my time was spent outdoors. I hated my mother's house. Everything that went on there didn't include me. I was fed, but it was mostly me sitting at the table with them, like I was a guest invited over to watch some cheesy television show about a happy family. I could pretend (if I wanted to) that I was a part of this family, but I knew there was something in the way keeping that from being true. Much as I might have wanted to be a member of the Walton or Brady family, I could no more join those families than I could my own.

Since I was outside most days and nights, I needed to learn to be a little more scrappy. I needed to fight. I quickly became known as someone who didn't shy away from conflict. Most of the bigger kids wanted a piece of the new guy, which made me fair game to one and all. I had two or three fights a week, usually with kids bigger and older than me, either because I was new, small, easy to make fun of, the girls liked me more, or because of nothing at all.

I was drawing when I heard the knock at the door.

Who could that be? I wondered.

We rarely got visitors. My mother was not very liked in the neighborhood, and most of the people would stay away unless they absolutely had to visit.

I walked over to the window and saw a neighborhood kid.

"What do you want, James?" I asked.

"You coming out?" He responded. "Let's hang out."

I knew James from school. He lived in the building across from us with his older brother and sisters. They were a large family that all stuck together. He seemed cool, so I put on my sneakers and ran out the door.

As I headed out, I remembered my mother's admonition: if I wasn't back in the house by 8 PM, the door would be locked.

If James and I stayed out late while getting up to some mischief, it wouldn't be the first time I was locked out, and it wouldn't be the last either.

We went down to the other side of the projects, talking and bothering the girls that were outside. James viewed himself as some kind of Casanova, believing that every girl liked him, but they only bothered giving him the time of day because every girl wanted to join his sisters' clique since they were cool and could fight.

It was getting late and the weather was starting to turn. Snow was on the way. There were voices around--other people hanging out. Older guys.

They used to stay in the hallways of the buildings, especially when it got colder. I used to hang out there and just observe what was going on. I earned a bit of respect from some of the older guys by holding my own when a couple of them had fought me. It didn't get me much more than a nod when I walked by, but that was good enough for me.

I was thinking about this when James called me out.

I thought that James had wanted to hang out, that we might start to be friends. But apparently, because I'd recently beaten the shit out of a kid named Mark earlier in the week, James was out for revenge. The only reason why I fought Mark was because he and three others decided they wanted to jump me. I rumbled with them. I'm not gonna pretend that I'm Rambo, but I managed to keep my head above water. The four of them were trying really hard to work me over, but I focused my attention on Mark.

James wanted to get retribution for his friend.

Everyone recognized that a fight was brewing, but it took me a while to realize what was happening.

As I tried to figure out what James was going on about, I saw Mario, another fake pretty-boy leaning on one of the railings on the steps leading into a building. He thought of himself as the hottest thing on two legs just because he was mixed Latino and black. Girls liked how he looked, but he wasn't anything special.

As he walked down the stairs, he turned and nodded to James as he passed me. Before I knew what was happening, he grabbed me around the waist. Put me in a headlock as I struggled to get free, then started raining blows on me.

I grabbed him and we both went down on the concrete. Blood dripped from my ear, but I didn't care. I wanted to knock this guy out.

The fists kept coming and he talked a lot of shit.

I got my legs around him to keep him from getting up.

As we tussled, the windows opened up in the buildings around us.

People laughed as they watched. Probably at me, but

maybe at both of us for being idiots and fighting in the middle of everything. Some people started screaming at Mario. "Get off him, he's just a kid!"

Mario didn't listen.

After what felt like an eternity, I did the only thing I could think of to make him let go of my head.

I bit the shit out of him.

Like he was made of Hamburger Helper.

He screamed. "He bit me! He bit me! Get him off!"

His grip loosened, but I kept biting. Started throwing punches. I wasn't going to back down that easily. Finally, someone else came, pulled me off, dragged me across the ground, and threw me in a heap. I lifted my shirt to look at the damage while Mario screamed and cried.

Not one to hang around in these situations, I got up and started running back to my building.

My mother was standing at the door.

Not the door to our apartment--that would have been great--but the door to our building. I knew that I was in a world of trouble. My mother, the same woman who did any and everything she could to give me grief, wouldn't want to hear that I was protecting myself. She wouldn't care that I had school in the morning. She wouldn't do anything but scowl and get belligerent. And when she got belligerent, it meant screaming and yelling, sometimes physical punishment.

I suffered through her abuse that night, and woke up the next morning with my ear throbbing. I'd have to endure the pain. My mother would do nothing to help. For better or for worse, all the years of enduring torment at the hands of my mother, or because of her apathetic attitude toward me, prepared me to be indifferent to pain years later.

I headed to the shower. I wanted to wash the previous night off of me. As I walked by the mirror in the bathroom, I glanced over. My ear didn't look too bad, though it was still swollen and felt hot.

Despite what you might be thinking, I wanted to go to school that morning. I liked to learn, and caught on to things quickly. I liked most of my teachers. I liked to read. I had a desire to better myself through knowledge. I also had a gift: if I read something, learned something, or heard something, I had a very hard time forgetting it.

As I left the shower, I heard a knocking on the front door.

My mother already left for work, and everyone else was already gone.

The knocking continued.

"I'm coming," I said.

I put on pants and walked to the door. When I looked through the peephole, I couldn't believe who I saw. A girl with long, dark, wavy hair.

Mario's younger sister, Rose.

Very few people actually talked to her because they were afraid of her brother. She was about two years older than me, short, thick, and--in my humble estimation--very pretty.

"What do you want?" I gruffly asked.

"I need to talk to you." Rose sounded sweet and kind. "I owe you an apology."

"For what?"

"My brother."

I unlatched the chain and opened the door for her. My mother would have had a fit if she knew I let someone in the house. A small laugh escaped my lips as I smiled at the fact that my mother wouldn't know.

"Look," Rose said. "I just want you to know that my brother was wrong for what he did, but he paid for it cause he had to get a tetanus shot for that bite. It's gonna leave a vicious scab."

I wasn't proud of what I'd done, but nothing is fair in a fight with the entire neighborhood watching.

Before I could even fully think that, I felt Rose's hand on my swollen ear. It was gentle. It felt nice to have someone carefully touch a spot that hurt, instead of making it worse. I wanted to move away, but her hand felt like it was healing me. Even after we parted ways, I could still feel her touch on my ear for hours.

Finally, I turned away, smiling to myself so she couldn't see, and put on my sneakers. I grabbed her hand as I went to the door. "Let's go."

"Where are we going?" Rose asked.

"To school."

CHAPTER TWO-AND-A-HALF

JIMMY & FYNGAZ

I often used different names when I was doing jobs elsewhere around the country. I didn't want people to recognize who I was immediately. Letting them figure it out as I worked, afterwards, or at some other point was part of the fun. I had reputations that preceded me pretty much wherever I went. But it's not good for business if everyone knows your name.

Jimmy was a sobriquet that I used whenever out of town. It was common for me to take on different names to conceal my actual identities. I wanted to be able to go around places where I may only have been known by reputation and act with impunity. Sometimes, things could get very volatile.

Many locals in places outside of New York didn't take kindly to people from the city. They liked to believe they ran their area. Truth was, they did, but only if we weren't there. Generally, we let them believe they were in charge, that they were safe from us because of their own power.

This mentality made them angry whenever we came down

looking for money, or women to sleep with. They didn't care for us doing that. Sometimes they needed to be taught a lesson.

There were some who appreciated guys like us. We brought down larger quantities of drugs and sold them at significantly cheaper prices. This was a boon. I had some connections with these people and often worked with them. They knew my actual name. Others I dealt with on occasion, specifically those who didn't like me or my New York friends, mostly knew me as Jimmy.

Jimmy was a legend.

Jimmy's reputation was much the same as my own in New York. People didn't want to cross Jimmy. But Jimmy was a generic enough name that it lent me a level of both anonymity and safety. People trusted Jimmy, because Jimmy could be anyone.

Was I that Jimmy? Who knows?

Fyngaz was a different story.

A more innocent, kind of silly, story.

As a young kid, most of my friends' parents liked me. I was polite, respectful, and good-natured. If friends invited me over to their houses, their parents were usually glad to see me, but they always made sure to take precautions when I would visit. Expensive items, family heirlooms, anything valuable, all of these items would be placed somewhere out of my reach.

Not because I had sticky fingers, I don't believe in stealing from innocent people, but my fingers were decidedly slippery. I was clumsy. I could be drinking something from a glass and my attention would be elsewhere. Before I knew what was going on, the glass would be in a thousand pieces on the floor, or the contents would wind up all over the couch I was sitting on. If the glass was on a table, I'd invariably knock it over with a swing of my arm. If it was in my hands, that might even be worse. It would just slip, or I'd get distracted by something else and completely forget that I needed to keep holding on to what was in my hand. No matter how much I tried, I couldn't stop it from happening. At first, people found it cute.

Oh, look at that, they'd say, *how adorably clumsy.*

Soon though, everyone from my friends' parents to my own family would start putting their breakable valuables out of my reach. Local restaurants hated when I'd walk in.

Strangers, friends, family, everyone knew the clumsiness I possessed.

That might have been enough to eventually have the name disappear. If I was just clumsy, eventually I might be able to get everyone to see the other traits I possessed, and have them start to refer to me by some other name. But I both solidified my reputation as a complete badass and permanently gave myself the name Fyngaz later in life.

At fifteen years old, I started carrying a gun. I didn't just have one--I'd mess around with lots of guns.

There was a time shortly after I started carrying when my sister Debbie ran to me crying. A boy in her high school tried to talk to her. When she refused, he slapped her.

I was furious.

Debbie didn't need to be my sister for me to see the problem. She could have been a girl I knew from the neighborhood. Hell, she could have been a random stranger, and I probably would have stood up for her. Especially if the circumstances were as she described.

I grabbed my gun--a 38 automatic--and went to her school. Waited outside for when the students would be let out at three. Debbie was one of the first to come pouring out the doors.

She saw me across the street and ran over.

I asked her to point the boy out. "Just going to have a talk with him."

After a few minutes passed, Debbie pointed at the boy as he left school.

I nodded, told her to head home, and approached him.

He looked older than I was, but I didn't care. I was so tall for my age, I regularly passed for someone in his twenties.

I asked him about the incident. Explained who I was. Made it clear that I only wanted to talk. I could tell he thought the situation should be resolved in a different way. His boys seemed to think the same thing, as one tried to circle around and get behind me.

I pulled out the gun and turned, pistol-whipping the friend. If they wanted to play that way, then we were going to play that way.

He fell to the ground, bleeding from his forehead.

I turned back to the original guy who slapped my sister.

He ran down the street.

I fired the gun twice and hit him both times directly in the ass.

He fell to the ground, grabbing his cheeks like he was ready to spread them, and the crowd outside the school screamed.

I walked calmly away from the school as if nothing had happened, and by the time I was a few blocks away, I hauled ass and got somewhere else. I certainly wasn't stupid enough to stay near the scene. And even though I knew there were ways to figure out who fired the gun, I held on to it.

Things were different in those days. It was rare for a young kid to be carrying a gun. Arguments, especially among young kids, were settled with fisticuffs. If you had a gun, inevitably, you were talked about and feared. Also, surprisingly, a lot of girls tried getting to know me because of it. Especially Debbie's friends.

Time went by and no one questioned me. Nothing seemed to come out of shooting this kid.

They say that once you get away with shooting someone, every argument eventually reaches a point where you pull out a gun. With me, however, I'd pull the gun, and then the trigger. My reputation for having an itchy trigger finger traveled. I wasn't aiming to kill--not all the time--but what good is it to constantly pull a gun and never use it? All that gets you is a reputation of carrying a piece, but being afraid to use it. I wasn't having that.

As my reputation grew, so did my ego.

Everybody wanted to act as if they knew me, like we had always talked and were thick as thieves. I was getting money because people started trusting me with odd jobs here and there. I dressed in the latest fashions, wore expensive jewelry, and carried myself like a big deal.

I believed I was untouchable.

Until the day that I was touched.

I was out of town, hustling, making good money. I was fifteen and selling some serious weight in Richmond, Virginia. As a side hustle, though, I'd occasionally rob some people who carried their own weight, or who had jewelry that I wanted.

This particular night, I'd just snatched some chains and rings, and was walking down the street feeling really good after growing my collection, my ego making me feel like I was ten feet tall.

A guy jumped from the shadows carrying a sawed-off shotgun. He aimed at my chest. Ordered me not to move. Or else.

"I mean it, motherfucker," he said. "You move and I'll blow your fucking head off."

I was dumbfounded.

Here I am, top dog, and this guy thinks he can take me? A nobody thief had the balls to approach me. I couldn't believe it.

"The fuck you will," I replied.

He smiled and aimed at my head.

"You got any idea who I am?" I asked, unfazed by the gun.

"Yeah," he answered. "I know who you are."

I smiled.

"You're some stupid motherfucker," he continued, "who's gonna give me all his shit."

At that moment, I realized that my reputation had not yet traveled down to Virginia. In New York I might be a scary nigga, but here, on some random street, in a city five hundred miles away, I was just another vic who got caught slipping.

I looked at the gun. The two barrels were once again pointed at my chest. I didn't have much choice if I wanted to live.

"Hate to disappoint." I flashed a wicked grin. "You ain't getting any of my shit."

His face changed briefly, surprised I was unbothered by the gun. If he wanted my gold, he was going to have to shoot me. I was hoping he would be too pussy and back down, but his face lit with sheer joy at the prospect of shooting me. I had two choices: die or do something drastic.

It was a perfect storm of things happening.

I knew how shotguns work. I knew that the shells are loaded with tiny ball bearings. I knew that when the shells explode out of the ends of the barrels, the ball bearings spread out. I knew that I didn't give the bearings a chance to go anywhere except directly into the ends of my hand as I reached and stuck two fingers into the gun--one for each barrel.

He pulled the trigger.

Fire shot out the back of the shotgun as its hammer struck the ring pin.

I saw the gun recoil from the explosion of the gunpowder. I saw the shockwave made as the explosion broke the sound barrier. I saw my family--Mama, my aunts, my mother, my half-brothers, everyone. Everything was in slow motion.

Until it wasn't anymore.

One of my fingers was entirely gone. Obliterated. Nothing left.

The other was flesh and bone and pulp, hanging there. Some of the spray from the shell got out and destroyed my left leg's calf muscle. I was a mess.

But I was alive.

The guy had no more shells. He saw me still standing, looking like something out of a horror movie, and didn't even try to pursue his goal, turning tail and running.

I was a little short on body parts, but I had my life. I had my jewelry. I was alive. No one was going to fuck with someone who had the balls to do what I just did.

From then, the nickname Fyngaz had taken on a completely different meaning.

3

———

STREETS

ROSE WAS my first American experience. I loved walking to school with her and seeing the looks people gave us. Nobody could believe she wanted to be with me, yet there we were, her and I walking hand in hand.

We were incredibly protective of each other. When I started spending less time at school, she got angry. I tried to explain it wasn't my fault. I was suspended regularly due to the fights I'd get into. The school administration simply didn't want me around.

But like Rose, there were a few teachers who took an interest in me. They recognized I was a smart kid with a desire to learn. I appreciated their interest, but I needed to keep my image as it was. Not that I was looking to fight. It was often someone else trying to pick one with me. It didn't matter though. Rose was tired of it, and I was drifting away from her. I made new friends, and hung out with different crowds. The writing was on the wall for Rose and I.

Later in life, when I wound up moving to New Jersey, that was it. Life became completely different.

I left New York because I was filled with such anger and hatred toward my mother that I could never be a good son. I never felt the love I grew accustomed to when living at Mama's house. I missed that love. An unconditional, wonderful feeling. In my mother's house, there were a million little conditions that I needed to abide by in order to afford a small percentage of that love.

I hated it.

It numbed me to love. Where I should have been accepting it whenever given, I shunned it away, and brushed it off as weakness. In the world I'd soon inhabit, being weak wouldn't help me. Not at all.

Only the strong would survive.

So my life changed. I grew up as the product of my environment and the people around me. I understood the importance of looking out for myself. If something would benefit me, it was worth my time. If there was no personal benefit, I wasn't interested. This kind of mindset led to some less than savory decisions, but in my youth, I certainly didn't care.

I was invincible.

I could not be defeated.

I was a success.

THE ALARM CLOCK on my dresser read: 8:00 P.M.

Although a bit drowsy, I was ready for the night's activities. While most people are cuddled up cozy in their beds, fast asleep, I was up taking care of my business. And when most people got up to go about theirs, I was nestled at home with the woman I was in a steady relationship with.

Inez and I didn't keep the same hours. As I was getting up, she just got into bed. We understood each other and made time for our relationship. I was cautious about love, as I always had been, but this was as close as I'd gotten in a very long time.

"How you feelin?" I asked.

There was a glint of anger in her green eyes as she looked at me. "I'm not happy with what you're doing. I'll live. But I'm not happy about it."

I shrugged and flashed her a winning smile.

"I'm glad you keep me away from all that," she said, "but I'm not gonna pretend I like it."

I chuckled and swung my legs out from under the blanket. It was getting dark outside. On the way to the bathroom, I wrapped Inez up in my arms and kissed her. She smiled at me as I closed the door.

In situations like this, I liked taking a cold shower. It cleared my head and helped me focus. Invigorated me.

Washed and dried, I dressed in my all black outfit for the night.

"Should I expect you back sometime tonight?" Inez asked. "Or until I get back from work?"

"I'm really not sure," I said. "I shouldn't be long. I've got a few stops to make and a few things to do."

She nodded stiffly.

I couldn't blame her. As much as I was going to miss her, I couldn't tell her I would probably be gone for a few days. She'd get upset. We'd argue about how my business interfered with our relationship. I didn't have the energy for that right then. Or anymore, quite honestly.

Inez was possessive. It didn't bother me, but I had to do what was best for me. I needed to look out for myself.

I smiled at her, blew a kiss, and walked out the door.

We lived in a nice area. It was populated with working-class people, leading their own respective lives. There were manicured lawns, a community gym with a pool, and a generally quiet atmosphere. People mostly kept to themselves, but there was community spirit.

I moved quickly to my car--a two-tone cashmere Acura LS sedan that changed colors as day shifted to night--doing my best to appear inconspicuous. I didn't need attention, but I wanted to make sure that I wasn't being followed or observed. Once at my car, I jumped in and started the ignition. I didn't like to wait for the car to warm up. I was always antsy to get on the move.

I stopped at a random CVS. That was my typical modus operandi. I'd get about a mile or so from home and then check to make sure everything was all right with the car. It was never the same place, and it was never in a pattern. I didn't want to fall into any specific habits when it came to my nocturnal activities. In my line of work, predictability was a killer.

While sitting in the parking lot, my beeper went off.

I saw the code and immediately drove to a payphone. I couldn't understand what the urgency was, especially since it was only a few minutes since I checked in with my bredrin. Regardless, I got to the payphone, dropped a dime, and called the number.

After two rings, Scully Dread answered.

"Wah gwan bredrin?" I said.

"Yo, big man," he said, "you need to link us now and mek sure dat you bring some Fronto when you come."

Asshole, I thought. *This is the emergency?*

I laughed off my annoyance.

Of course he wanted Fronto. It's a type of tobacco leaf used to roll weed. It burns real slow and lets you get the full effect of the ganja. But when Scully talks like that, there's something on his plate. Maybe it was urgent.

I drove to a store I knew carried the Fronto leaf. It was in the direction I was headed anyway, so it was no big deal to make the stop. After being buzzed in, I headed to the store's back where I grabbed a case of Heiniken and Guinness. If they wanted to smoke, they probably wanted to drink too.

At the counter, I asked for Fronto and a pack of Craven A cigarettes. These were the Newports of Jamaica. While I didn't smoke cigarettes regularly, I would indulge on occasion. I figured that meeting up with these cats, especially if Scully had something on his plate, was an occasion.

Before reaching Sully's, I stopped at another payphone. Dialed a number I rarely called. After three rings, a woman answered. Despite living in the United States for years, her accent was still thick as if she just immigrated.

"Hello?" My mother said.

I didn't respond.

"Hello? Hello?" She continued. "Is that you?"

I hung up.

Back in my car, I opened the pack of cigarettes, took one out, lit it, and deeply inhaled.

Why do I even bother? I thought. *Love cannot survive this absence of memories. I should have no interest in her.*

I flicked the cigarette out the window and pulled off, leaving those thoughts behind.

Now was not the time to get caught up in the past. There was a whole other world that existed in the night I needed to attend. As one part of the city prepared to sleep, another side geared up for activity. This was the time for hustlers, card-sharps, gamblers, prostitutes. This was the time when adventurous, working-class people would step out looking to see how the other half lives. This was vice time.

It was around ten when I arrived at the building and parked in front. It was in the downtown area, where there was little worry about being seen, a key reason why we picked this location. It was an easily accessible, centrally located, busy area where there was less chance of anyone noticing us coming and going.

None of us lived there; it wasn't exactly what you'd call homey. Sure, every now and then we'd bring some chick we met at a club or get comfortable enough to relax for a bit, but we mainly used this place to conduct clandestine business. Aside from that, we didn't spend much time there.

Outside the building, I noticed a woman by the front door. This was her territory.

"Anything I need to know about?" I asked as I got closer to her.

"Nah. Just the regular shit," she said. "Saw some of your buddies go in a while ago. Didn't see them leave."

I fished out a ten-spot and handed it to her. "Make sure that you keep your eyes open for me."

She pocketed the bill. "When do I ever have them closed?"

I reached the third floor, and instead of using my keys, I knocked. The little bit of noise I could make out through the steel door came to an utter stop. When knocking again, I banged a rhythm on the door, a code.

"Ah, who dat?" I'd know Scully's voice anywhere. He always made himself seem bigger than life. But underneath that, he was incredibly loyal, serious, and contemplative.

"Ah mi mon," I said. "Open up di door nuh man."

This was a little ritual we both went through. The hesitancy and the little bit of the back-and-forth between us has saved our lives on several occasions.

Scully opened the door.

As I walked in, I noticed the unmistakable smell of what goes for incense in this place: ganja smoke. Laughter came from the back room; everyone was already there. Usually, I try to be the last person to arrive, but the first to leave once business has been concluded. I like to be by myself. I don't need to spend extra time around these guys. That's not to say I didn't like them, but I preferred my own company. Or the company of a woman.

The den was filled with marijuana smoke. I threw the Fronto leaf on the table. Everyone looked at it, then me, then burst out laughing. They seemed to have been partying all night. At this point, they were just letting the entertainment die down so we could get to business. Taking the cue, I headed into the other room--where we usually conduct business--and waited.

One by one they trickled in. Finally, we could begin.

"Okay, let's get this over with," Scully said

"Nah, tek your time, bredrin," I said. "No need for haste. I've got plenty of time."

At that, NicNic stood up and placed something on the table. A key. NicNic was not a very loquacious person. He always said as little as possible, but was exceptionally attentive in the areas he needed to be. For him to bring that much attention to himself surprised us.

Everyone at the table seemed to know what the key was for, like they had discussed it beforehand.

Meanwhile, I was at a loss. "How'd you get your hands on this? Who did it belong to?"

Everyone looked at me, silently.

"Scully, tell mi wah gwan and wen did you make the decision to nyam de bwoy dem food?" My Jamaican patois would come out when I was caught off guard.

"You already know that it was in the works," Scully responded, "and we know how you operate."

I had three specific and strict rules. If all three cannot be met or guaranteed, then I do not participate.

First, the job needs to be worth it. At a minimum, it must provide me with enough money for bail and a lawyer, and set me up for a period of time that commensurates the risk. Second, I have to be able to get away with it, barring that rule number one guaranteed enough money to hire someone to fight the case. Third, I need to know what it will cost. If I need to outlay more than I think the job is worth, I'm not interested.

"Okay, hold on," I said. "Let me think this out cause it seems as if the decision was already made without me."

I ripped off a piece of the Fronto leaf and began rolling a big-head spliff. Once finished, I slid it behind my ear and took out the pack of cigarettes, standing it up on the table. No one touched it.

I surveyed each man at the table, trying to gauge something that I couldn't even explain. They knew what I was doing. That, I'm sure of.

"Listen," I said, "if you want me to get this right, I need to know all the angles, as well as what I'm up against."

I locked eyes with NicNic.

He talked. "I've been seeing a woman who is supposed to be Sprag's baby mother. It's a known fact he's fucking her cousin. Well, not really known--I put it out there--but now she's disgruntled and wants to punish him for his indiscretions. She asked if I could accommodate. Of course, I said yes, and even went so far as to request easy access to the house where he makes his money, the same place we talked about robbing anyway. Ah long time dem bwoy deh ligit juk, and now we have a key to their gates. Now, there's one stipulation I agreed to, and so must you. We can not kill or seriously hurt them."

So that's what I'm looking at?

The key to our next move, if it was agreed upon.

"NicNic, I respek you, rudie," I said, "but I already see a number of flaws, as well as the potential for failure."

One being that no one can predict the outcome of a robbery, especially against violent yardmen.

"We can't guarantee none of the stipulations you agreed to," I stated. "Shit, it might be one of us who get killed or seriously hurt. Have you forgotten what happened to Eyelash?"

Eyelash was the younger brother of a close friend. He was brought onto a robbery that was supposed to be a soft target, a sort of training and introduction to the heist game. He was killed his first time out.

"Did you even consider that the baby mother is a liability?" I asked. "If we're forced to hurt someone, there's no telling if she'll decide to tell Sprag who robbed him to get back in his good graces. That's something you must worry about, cause if it comes to that, you will be the only one that can be identified, and that's just to name a few dilemmas."

As he opened his mouth to speak, I held up a hand to cut him off.

"Hold on, let me think, cause I have to make sure that I secure me."

"You already know what it is," Alley interjected. "All we need from you is how we get in and out with the minimum amount of risk."

I could always count on Alley to put it to me plainly. There were lots of guys who tried beating around the bush and gave me a whole elaborate story. Not Alley.

"If we get this off," Scully added, "we will be able to chill for a while and put whatever we get from this into what we already got."

I paused. "You all know how I feel about this."

Everyone nodded.

"After this," I said, "we need to lay low for a bit. We've got to take a break. This is some hazardous work. It's not every time we're gonna get it right. If this is what I think it is though, the reward definitely outweighs the risk."

In agreement, we jumped into action.

4

———

THE LICK

THERE WAS a flurry of activity in the apartment as we finished our preparations.

This was a job we discussed before. We had a plan in place, contingencies, and contingencies for those contingencies. We knew pretty much what to expect, so there was little more to talk about, but we were all still acting cautiously.

I headed down to the garage and went straight for a Nissan Stanza I kept near the building. Before jumping in, I changed its license plates and obscured some of the numbers. The target was another apartment complex.

I parked outside, with a straight view of the designated apartment. It was midnight on a Friday. My hope was that the occupants of the complex were winding down from a hard day's hustle, or they were already asleep.

I couldn't place it, but something felt like it was missing. It kept nudging and tickling my brain. Usually, I call off a job if I get a feeling like this, but we were already set up and everything seemed good to go. We had a car parked two blocks down with the best driver from the group. I brought an extra guy with us, in spite of others grumbling about having an extra mouth to feed. Once I made it clear that if he wasn't in then neither was I, they quickly quieted and agreed to his addition, though I'm sure a couple did so begrudgingly.

I was a natural leader. It always seemed to fall into my lap. I never asked to be in charge, I just found myself in that position. I could have made the call, right then and there, and nixed this job for the night. But the nagging feeling in my head wasn't strong enough to pull the cord.

I shook off the feeling and kept watch.

A Toyota Cressida pulled up in front of the building. A guy stepped out and leaned into the passenger side window to talk to some girl. I knew him very well. Sprag was an incredibly violent man, but had a weakness for girls. Around them, he tended to let his guard down.

Sprag being here was not necessarily good for our plans.

We didn't anticipate his arrival when devising the plan and its contingencies. Even still, I knew we'd be able to get things done. There would be three people inside. A fourth would complicate the matter, but I wasn't prepared to abort the plan.

As I watched Sprag talk to the girl, I realized that things might actually work to our advantage. NicNic was on the second floor waiting for the go ahead. The others were already in place. Sprag being here might help make things move a little more smoothly, but it all depended on NicNic's ability to improvise.

I slowly exited my car, then speed walked across the street, hoping that NicNic had an inkling of what was going on down here. As I reached the entrance, I slowed down. In this line of work, timing was everything.

Sprag bounded up the steps two at a time.

As he rounded the third floor landing, NicNic came swiftly around the corner, black ski mask on.

Sprag didn't hear him.

Quiet as a mouse, NicNic got behind Sprag and grabbed him around the waist. "Pussy, don't move or you're dead."

Sprag turned and came face to face with a nine Taurus pointed at his forehead.

I pulled on my hoodie to obscure my face as I stepped up and grabbed Sprag around the neck, whispering in his ear, "Stand in front of the door and knock. You flinch or give any indication that something is amiss, I'm gonna shoot you ina your wood and you won't be able to service dem gyal deh weh you ah run round wid, you zimi?"

He nodded.

"If you mek one bloodclot move fi dat deh gun deh weh you have, I will mek sure you nuh live fi see mawnin'." People knew I'm from the islands, but because I spent so much time in the United States, most people only heard my American English. Speaking patois was like wearing a second mask that hid my identity.

Sprag put himself in front of the door as NicNic and I stood off to either side. He knocked. The door clicked open and Sprag bolted for it and tumbled through shouting, "Lock di door! Lock di bombaclot door! Robber bwoy dem deh bout!"

They tried to slam the door shut. I stuck my foot out, keeping it open. NicNic and I leveraged the door open, swinging it into the face of the idiot still standing there.

Rushing inside, I grabbed Sprag from behind. "Come here, bwoy." I pulled him toward me. "Mi nuh tell you nuh fi try any bloodclot ting."

I clocked him in the head with the butt of my gun and down he went.

NicNic secured the other people in the apartment.

With Sprag out of commission for the moment, I walked to the stereo system, pulled a Maxwell cassette from my pocket, and dropped it in the slot. Shabba Ranks pumped out of the speakers.

Ting ah ling ah ling, school bell ring, knife and fork ah fight fi dumpling.

NicNic waited for me in the living room, holding the others at gunpoint while I checked the complex's hall to ensure no one heard the commotion. Spotting Screw--another member of our crew--coming up the stairs carrying duffel bags, I left the apartment's door unlocked and came back inside.

When we all gathered in the living room, I spoke. "Listen to me. This is gonna take no more than ten minutes. You make it take any longer than that, I'm gonna be forced to use extreme tactics to get back on schedule."

They nodded.

"I'm gonna ask you some things, and you're gonna answer me. It's as simple as that. Follow?"

They nodded again.

"Great," I said. "Where is the money?"

They looked around, doing their best to act confused.

"Don't tell me there is none, because I know there is."

"There isn't," one said, a guy named Neville. "Really. When you busted in, where do you think Sprag was coming from? He already dropped it all off."

I picked up a cushion off the couch and held it to the guy's head. Pressed the gun's muzzle into it. "So far, that's taken three minutes. You've got seven left. Still wanna tell me there's no money?"

Neville hesitated. Eyes larger than saucers, he looked at the other guys, trying to call my bluff. At the rate time was ticking, he was going to learn that I never bluffed. I could tell he was just about ready to break.

"You've got two minutes left." I cocked back the hammer.

Finally, the pressure of the situation made Nevil and his bladder crack.

"It's in the bathroom. In the drop ceiling. Just push up on the tile over the toilet."

I walked into the bathroom, leaving NicNic and Screw to keep an eye on the boys out there. Following Nevil's instructions, I found a black leather satchel. Inside was a .357 Python sitting on stacks of cash.

Leaving the satchel on the floor, I returned to the living room as Stag stirred awake and motioned Screw into the bathroom. "Empty the bag on the floor and make sure there's nothing else in there."

Facing our captives, I asked, "Where is the product?"

"Man, you askin' for what we ain't got," Sprag said.

"The ten minutes are up, and what I found in the bathroom really isn't worth my time," I said.

"Come on, man. You already tek de fuckin' money. You askin' for what ain't here."

"Clyde," NicNic said to me, knowing not to use my real name, "we've already been here too long. We should get going."

"You're right. But not before I get what we came here for." I went up to Sprag and pistol whipped him over and over and over again.

Blood squirted everywhere.

Nevil squirmed as he watched. Then screamed, "It's under di stove. Under di stove!"

Fortunately, Shabba Ranks was louder than Neville.

At the stove, I slid out the bottom and reached my hand underneath. Felt around. Touched something solid.

My first discovery was stacks of cash and four pounds of weed, both tightly wrapped in plastic. Thinking I might be done, I started pulling my hand out. Then I brushed against something else. Pulled it out.

Along with the cash and weed, two kilos of cocaine and a gun had been stashed in the hiding spot.

"Yo, Squallah." That was Screw's sobriquet for this job.

He ran over and started loading his duffel bags.

I turned to NicNic.

"My yout gwan. Mi ah go link you when I touch. I have it from here."

Screw was already out the door with the bags by the time NicNic started backing up, still aiming his gun at our targets. Once NicNic was out the door, I was alone with them.

I kept my gun trained on them as I left, closed the door, then ran down the steps, clearing the last flight in one single leap. I was out the front door and down the block back to my Nissan in a flash. I jumped in, drove around the block once, passing the transfer car to make sure the crew was also on their way, then sped onto the highway. I had other things to take care of right then, but I wasn't concerned about the money or drugs. They'd be safe with the rest of the crew.

I still had this gnawing feeling in my gut while heading to my next destination. I expected to be there for a while, but there was no better time to take care of this. I needed to.

I turned left at a familiar exit, drove down South Harrison St., then parked outside the 106 building. Inside the lobby, I went up the staircase to the 4th floor and knocked twice on Nicole's door, an older woman who lived in the apartment. I could always talk to her without worrying about our conversation being repeated, and she was very discreet with dialings. The door opened, and I was greeted with a smile that I returned. I walked past her into the living, sat on the couch, and took out my gun, placing it on the table.

"It's that serious?" She asked.

"Not really," I replied, "but one can never be too cautious."

"Around here, you are safe."

"For now."

Nicole's eyebrows knitted together. "What's on your mind?"

"There's this guy I want to link, and I want you to help me make it happen. I am sure he would be reluctant if I asked him directly, but if it comes from you, he will be interested enough to want to know the reason for my request."

"What about your trusted Demus?"

"First, my trusted Nicole."

"Yeah, coming from a man who trust no one."

I smirked. No more words needed to be stated. We both came to an understanding.

Reaching for my gun, I rose.

"Hungry?" Nicole asked.

"I'll take you up on that next time. I just ate a belly full."

I took the elevator down, jumped in my car, and started mentally preparing myself for the trip to the apartment. After I got my cut, it'd be time to put the next phase of my plan into effect.

Hopefully, she'd be out there.

5

___

RAGE

I FOUND myself in the principal's office.

Again.

I sat on the wooden bench, for what felt like hours, in the administrative office with my head down. The old-lady secretary, Ms. Nivens (probably Mrs. Nivens, but we all could never imagine her married), kept looking up and smiling at me. She considered me a "good kid," but disapproved of how often I found myself sitting across from her, waiting for the principal and one other person that needed to be there.

My mother.

When arriving, she immediately went into a rant about my behavior. It started quietly, but it built up steam quickly.

Ms. Nivens looked up and asked my mother to keep it down. "This is a place of business."

My mother looked away with a sigh.

Ms. Nivens winked at me, sympathetically.

We were finally brought into the principal's office. With a new audience, my mother picked up her rant about my behavior, and I continued to study the floor. I made no eye contact, letting the anger flow through me, practicing what Mama had taught me. Mama sensed that I was a methodical young boy and always told me to control my emotions.

Don't let people be able to read you because you wear your emotions on your face, She said. *Your emotions speak to people without words.*

Meanwhile, I was getting a little bit of enjoyment out of the principal holding up a finger to silence my mother. My mother, the woman who believed she could do no wrong and was above everyone's authority, had no choice but to shut up and park her ass in a chair, just like me.

"I think you really hurt that boy," the principal said to me, shaking his head.

Earlier, the other students in class were laughing at me.

Tyrone pointed at me. *"Maybe we should teach him English, cause what he's saying isn't English. It sounds weird."*

The kids continued to laugh at Tyrone's taunts.

"I am speaking English. I have an accent. I come from some-where else, but I speak English." I was fuming. I was trying to keep my emotions in check, trying to not jump to any bad ideas, but everyone kept laughing.

This was the third day he was doing this. As much as I wanted to stay calm, I couldn't keep letting this happen. Like flipping on a light bulb, my mindset changed and I knew I needed to stop him, using whatever method available.

I tightened my grip on a pencil in my hand, walked straight to Tyrone, and jabbed him in the stomach.

The pencil went in, deep and clean. Tyrone immediately grabbed his stomach, doubled over, and fell down onto the classroom floor. In the space of a minute, our teacher left and came back with another instructor. While our teacher bent down and attended to Tyrone, I was grabbed and pulled out of the classroom. I could still hear Tyrone's screams from the classroom as I was dragged to the principal's office.

I was suspended.

Again.

As my mother dragged me back home, she continued the rant she'd begun in the principal's office. "I'm gonna beat your ass when we get home. Doing that to this innocent little boy. I can't believe you. Do you think this is what I brought you over to America for? How stupid are you? This is really how you want to start your life over here? By doing shit like this? By causing me three years of misery?"

By the time we reached home, I felt empowered. I turned to my mother and calmly said, with every shred of sincerity I could muster, "You should have left me with my grandmother."

I knew she'd be angry at this comment, but I didn't realize how much.

She started slapping me. The first one stung, unexpected, but the next several felt like nothing. I turned off my emotions and just let her go. Noticing this wasn't having any effect on me, she grabbed me by the arm and led me into my bedroom and slammed my fingers in the closet door.

I screamed out in pain.

When looking into the eyes of the woman I hated more than anything on the planet, I saw what could only be described as joy on her face. It disgusted me. For three years, I was locked out in the freezing cold because I was a minute late getting home, while my half-brothers were inside. Then there were days when I was locked out in the cold, even though I'd gotten home on time, only because she didn't want my half-brothers around me. They were given a key to come and go.

I was given nothing, forced to take refuge in the apartment complex laundry room. It was warm there. And more often than not, someone forgot their laundry that I'd use as a pillow or blanket.

At this time, I had a friend named Jenay. Her mother took pity on me, seeing the situation I was in, and helped me out whenever she could. Like Ms. Nivens, she knew I was a "good kid" with a bad circumstance.

To counter this, my mother started taking me to work with her when there was no school. She would leave me in the playground down the block from where she worked, rain or shine, for her entire shift.

Holidays were the worst. At Christmas my half-brothers got all the toys they wanted. They got warm sweaters, books, games, and anything else their hearts desired. I got nothing. Since she brought me to the United States and tore me away from all that was good in my life, she treated me like a stranger living in her house. Unless it was something I absolutely needed, or something that the school might judge her for not providing, I didn't get anything.

I managed by developing small hustles here and there. When it snowed, I would walk around in the white people's neighborhood offering to shovel driveways and sidewalks. They would pay me twenty dollars for my efforts, and some of the nicer houses would offer me hot chocolate. I never drank it, I developed a habit of needing to know where and how my food was prepared, but I did thank them. Afterwards, I'd take the money to the corner store near my apartment and buy an egg sandwich. It was one of my favorite meals. That or a thick, juicy hamburger. The rest of the cash would be stashed, in case I was locked out of my own house.

One day, school was closed, and for no explainable reason, rather than taking me to work with her, my mother left me in the apartment with my two half-brothers. Normally, they were miserable on the best of days, constantly reminding me that we were "just half-brothers, not real brothers." On this day, their abuse escalated.

I had already responded to the "half-brother" comment about a thousand times, telling them, in no uncertain terms, that we were not half-brothers. We were nothing to each other. And, after that, I would usually walk away. But I couldn't take any more.

I got up and walked toward them, trying to look as menacing as I possibly could.

They saw what was coming and did not back down. The youngest of the two ran at me with a pair of scissors. Stabbed me.

This set my rage on fire.

I pummeled my half-brothers. I beat the ever-loving shit out of them until the floor was a bloody mess. There was a scissor-sized hole on the side of my bicep and a few scratches here and there, but it was nothing compared to them.

Our mother came home, saw my half-brothers, and proceeded to beat me so badly I could barely move. The next day at school, the teacher sent me to the nurse, and Child Protective Services was called. CPS wanted to remove me from my mother's custody.

I was overjoyed, but I had no idea where I would go. Naturally I got nervous. I could survive on the streets if I needed to, but I didn't want to.

Jenay's mother who came to the rescue. She knew that I had an aunt who lived in New Jersey, and suggested that perhaps I could go live there. She did all the heavy lifting for me, making phone calls, getting my aunt to agree, and talking to CPS about it.

I knew it would be different, but I also knew that this aunt had also taken in one of my "sisters" (really another aunt) from when I lived with Mama. I was going to be able to go somewhere where I had a real sibling, not any of this "half-some-thing" nonsense.

My mother hated this particular aunt--her sister--and so, she asked me, on what would be the last day I would ever see her, "Are you sure you really want to go live with her?"

"Of course I do," I said. "There is nothing for me here."

I figured that would set her off, but she only seemed upset that her sister was taking custody of me.

By this time, though, I had been out of my mother's house for weeks, staying with a friend's family while everything was straightened out. Jenay's mother said she would have happily let me stay, but their apartment was too small for me. I under-stood. She had already done more than anyone else in the United States had for me.

My friend Leon, offered me a permanent place to stay with his grandma. I wouldn't need to leave New York. I considered it. Everything I knew about the United States was in New York. I didn't know anything about New Jersey besides the fact that people from New York made fun of people who lived there. Ultimately, I thanked Leon and his grandmother for the offer, but went to my aunt's house, deciding to be with family.

Years later, Leon was shot and killed during a botched robbery. If I was living there with him, I might have faced the same fate.

Jenay and her mother showed up at my house. Jenay's mother had agreed to drive me to New Jersey.

"Are you ready?" Jenay's mother asked.

Bag in my hand, I didn't even bother to look back at my "half-brothers," the place I lived for years, or my mother. It was satisfying to have that power over her. I nodded and walked out the door.

As we drove along the highway, I glanced out the window, trying to make sense of why I had to go through so much at such a young age. I should be enjoying life as a child. I should not have to fight to prove myself. I should not have grown up as fast as I did. But there I was. A survivor. I knew that much.

And I knew that I would continue to survive, no matter what life threw at me. As the car passed under a sign that read "Exit 10 - East Orange - Next Right," I hoped that New Jersey would be different.

6

———————

RELOCATION

IT WAS A VERY rainy day when the car got off of Exit-280 and onto the ramp that would take us to East Orange. After recollecting my thoughts, I looked around to see how different my new environment was from my old one. Based on what I heard, New York and New Jersey were like apples and oranges to each other. There were no big buildings or apartments built on top of storefronts, only a handful of traffic lights and wide roads. Out here, people lived in houses. People could afford houses. In New York, you had to be extremely wealthy to live in a private house.

Everything that I was used to was gone. It was all different, but I was excited about these changes and what this new life could offer.

After driving for another fifteen minutes, we pulled up at my aunt's house. Once the car stopped, I opened the door and took my few meager possessions. Jenay and her mother got out after me, and together, we walked to the door. I felt silly standing there with a baggie that contained three pairs of pants, some underwear, a few shirts, and the terribly light windbreaker that I was currently wearing.

Jenay's mother rang the doorbell.

There was some shuffling on the other side of the door. "Who's there?"

Jenay's mother pushed me forward and nodded.

"It's Leonel." I said, timidly. "Your nephew."

Jenay's mother smiled, proud of me.

The door opened and a girl around my age stood there. She wasn't my aunt. It wasn't possible.

"My mom and aunt are out getting some food right now," she said. "But they told me you were coming. I'm your cousin. Come in."

She led us all inside, then asked Jenay and her mother if they wanted anything to drink.

Jenay's mother explained that they needed to get back to the City.

My new cousin smiled as she patiently watched Jenay and her mother hug me goodbye, wishing me well. I embraced them both, unsure if I'd ever see either of them again, but exceptionally grateful for their kindness and help. Once back in the car, they waved to me as they drove off.

I dropped my bag on the floor and looked around. It wasn't different from an apartment, but it was a house. It was strange and familiar at the same time.

"Are you hungry?" My new cousin asked.

"Yeah," I sheepishly said.

She led me into the kitchen where she made us both peanut butter sandwiches.

"My name's Sophia," she told me. "I'm normally supposed to be in school, but my mother let me stay home so I could be here when you arrived. She wanted me to be here in case she needed to go out, and you got here while she was gone, that way there was someone who could let you in."

She talked and smiled a lot. It confused me at first, but I realized that she was excited about me being there. Her kindness was completely genuine, which made me feel comfortable.

Done eating, Sophia took my bag to the bedroom I would be staying in.

"You're going to be staying in the same room with my little brother." She set my bag down on a bed. "He's pretty cool as far as little brothers go, so you'll both probably get along okay. He's got a lot of toys and stuff to play with. He'll share with you, but you'll probably get some of your own pretty soon too."

After settling in, which really just amounted to putting my bag on the bed and looking around for a few minutes, I followed Sophia out to the living room and joined her on the sofa as she turned on the television. I'd only been in the house for two hours, maybe less, but I could already feel the difference between here and my mother's. This place felt more like Mama's house.

It was warm and cozy and inviting. I could let my guard down. Between the home's comfort and talking to Sophia, it felt like I lived in that house longer than I really had.

As time went by, I laid down on the couch, and before I knew it, I was asleep.

When my younger aunt Charm came home first, she woke me up by scooping me into her arms and spinning me around. It had been years since I saw her back when we lived at Mama's house. I was overjoyed.

Charm and I were the youngest kids at Mama's house, so we were always treated a little differently. Mama kept both of us under her wing more than other people living in her house. Because of that, Charm and I were as close as brother and sister.

I was so happy to see a familiar face, especially one I loved and cared for so much. From this alone, I got the immediate feeling that East Orange, New Jersey was going to be a good place for me.

"Tell me, little bro, how you feeling?" Charm asked, a smile on her face. "I know you miss Mama."

"Why can't we get her to come here and live with us?"

"She doesn't want to live in the United States. Plus, she's afraid to get on a plane. I told her a hundred times it's safe, but she still don't trust planes."

I laughed. "Tell her to get on a boat then."

"She don't wanna leave her home. Otherwise, she'd have been over here years ago. But we can always go back and visit her."

Before that moment, I never thought I'd see Mama again. Now, there was a chance that I could visit her. Immediately I fantasized about the market and the food and the smells and the whole of the islands.

Charm broke me from my reverie with some information that was both good and bad. "On Monday, we're going to sign you up for school. The school is just around the corner and a few blocks down. Between now and then, we're going to get you some school clothes."

I nodded.

I liked school. I really did. But I wasn't looking forward to being the new kid again. Especially here. This place was different from New York. My accent was bound to stick out here more than it did there.

As Charm spoke the front door opened.

My other aunt Mid came in, dropped what she had in hand, and rushed over to embrace me in the tightest hug I've had in my whole life. After years of ice from my mother, it was strange to have such a warm welcome. I didn't think it was possible for someone to be so happy to see me. Between my aunt, Charm, and my cousin Sophia, I'd never felt so accepted someplace except when I lived with Mama.

"Make yourself at home," she said when finally releasing me. "This is your home. Make yourself comfortable, relax, get used to the place. Just know that we all love you and we are so glad that you're here."

I had no idea how to respond. I smiled and nodded and sat back on the couch, just kind of looking around, with my hands folded on my lap. It was weird being there. But a good weird.

IT TURNED out that the area we lived in was predominantly made up of West Indian and Caribbean immigrants. Once I learned that I was probably going to hear a bunch of accents, and many of them being similar to my own, I was far less worried about standing out at school.

Our neighborhood was both quiet and had a lot going on. Most of the action was up the hill from where we lived on a road called Walnut Street. I knew from experience that once I was able to move around on my own, I'd really get a sense of how different it was from New York.

I went to Heart Middle School. There were three separate buildings that made up the school, much different from the one I went to in New York. Heart wasn't a great school--seemed to be more play than work--but it was extremely diverse. Because of what I'd already learned back in New York, I completed all of my school work and was eager to learn new things. Seeing that I was a good student, my teachers gave me extra credit work, and spent more one-on-one time with me. Eventually, I was skipped not once, but twice, to a higher grade level thanks to the extra attention.

This new environment, in all regards, was remarkable, and the first few weeks there were probably the most memorable times since I'd first arrived in the United States.

There was a lot of love in my aunts' house. My cousins and I got along really well. We laughed, played, joked, ate, and hung out together. We were like a real family.

My aunt worked two jobs, so we saw her infrequently. She would be gone for the night at one job, and when we got back from school, she would still be working. She struggled not just to provide a roof over our heads and food on the table, but also to keep us from seeing that we were a poor family living day to day. She wasn't playing pretend, but she wanted us to feel like anyone else. Everything she did was to make sure we had the best life possible, so that we could worry about what kids worry about, not adult concerns. As much as she struggled to do this, however, there were days when our table seemed a little barren. But while we didn't always eat our fill, we were never hungry.

I was fortunate that I was still able to visit New York often. I wanted to maintain the friendships I still had there. While I never visited my mother when I went to New York, I did, on occasion, wonder about her. From time to time, I would see her walking around the neighborhood, but if she saw me, she never let on, and I certainly never approached her. I treated her just like any other stranger on the street in the City.

EARLY ONE SATURDAY MORNING, while my aunt was still at work, I was outside the front of the house. My two cousins were still asleep, and I was growing bored sitting there waiting for something to do. I decided to venture out and explore the neighborhood.

I started walking in the direction of the corner store. It was a block or two away. As I turned the corner, I saw a group of kids around my age, sitting outside a house. As I walked past them, I heard one of them whisper to the group, "That's the new kid."

I pretended not to hear and kept walking, but I certainly did take notice of the two older girls hanging out.

As I walked out of the store a few minutes later, holding my purchase of a hot beef patty and drink, I saw the older girls again, separated from the group, as if they followed me down to the store. Inside, I smiled at this, but kept walking back to my house. I was a few yards past them when I heard one of the girls say, "He's cute."

I am going to like it here, I thought.

A few months later, I knew the ins and outs of living in New Jersey. I knew all about my neighborhood and knew a bunch of the kids, if not by name, by sight. I knew how to carry myself. I knew all the haunts and the pool rooms where I could hang out after school hours. I kept up with my education, but I was also focused on learning more about this other world I was seeing.

I felt it calling to me, and because of that, I wanted to know more and more about it.

One Saturday night, I was out wandering around looking for something to get into. It's true that my aunt did everything she could to take care of us all, but the one thing she wasn't able to do was provide a disposable income for us to buy things. I was fine with it, but I did like to have a few dollars in my pocket for snacks.

By this time, I was smoking weed regularly, and as I wandered around, I had a good sized joint in my pocket. I knew I was going to need something to snack on after smoking, so I stopped in the local Shoprite.

I didn't have two nickels to rub together, but I figured that didn't really matter. I grabbed a package of chicken bologna and some Vienna sausages and stashed them inside my windbreaker. I figured that would make a halfway decent snack after I smoked.

Little did I know that one of the store employees saw me do this.

Turns out he had been following me as I walked the aisles. The store had been robbed a few times in the last month, and I just happened to be stupid enough to try the same thing. They called the cops and I was arrested, but because I was a juvenile, there was little they could do except call my aunt. Shoprite got their property back, and my joint was confiscated, but otherwise, the cops figured it was probably easier for my family to dole out punishment.

I was embarrassed, even before my aunt came to pick me up. I was sitting, handcuffed to a bench, in a police station. I vowed, right then and there, never to steal anything again, or to be in a position where I couldn't afford to buy whatever I might want in life.

There are two things I despise: stealing and lying. What happened that night was a catalyst for a lot of things later in life, but it was the beginning of my belief that lying and stealing were wrong. Deeply and utterly wrong.

Had I been a smarter and wiser twelve year old, that experience may have shown and taught me that crime was wrong too, but that was not the lesson I learned at Shoprite. Instead, I faced more hardship later on--in part because of my choices, and in part because of circumstances outside my control--but this hardship helped me to become the man I am today.

A FEW WEEKS LATER, I was getting ready to go out. It was warm in the house and I was bored. My younger cousin Nor gave me a sad puppy dog look, desperately wanting to tag along. In other circumstances, I wouldn't have had a problem with it, but my aunt was protective and didn't let him go anywhere without her.

I shook my head and shrugged to apologize, then headed toward the door. As I opened it, I sensed that he was standing behind me. He wouldn't take no for an answer.

"Please," he whined.

I thought about it and sighed. "Just to the corner store and back, okay?"

He jumped for joy and I couldn't help but smile.

As we stepped onto the porch, however, the smile disappeared.

"Stay right here," I ordered. "Do not move. No matter what. You understand?"

He nodded, confused, but backed up and stood right by the door.

Across the street, I noticed a large group of kids standing there. I'd seen this play out before. I knew what was going to happen. New York and New Jersey kids were not completely dissimilar.

I went down the steps, motioning for my cousin to stay put, and headed in the direction of the store. No more than a few seconds must have gone by before one of the kids across the street ran over and got in my way. I stopped, sizing him up as several more of the kids joined us.

"You dissed my sister," he claimed.

"I don't even know your sister," I said.

He nodded back toward the street, and I spotted one of the older girls who called me cute outside the store.

"You did," she said. "I asked you your name and you just ignored me and kept walking."

I thought back to that day. I didn't remember hearing her call after me, but she might have. Either way, it didn't matter whether I'd heard her or not.

I started to walk away, but two guys blocked my path. I tried to get by them. Neither moved. Realizing I wouldn't get through, I spun off and walked over to the first guy who confronted me and punched him in the face.

He collapsed to the ground.

I got down to his level and started raining blows on his body. I punched, kicked, and grabbed, beating on him.

Eventually, I felt a hand around my waist.

I ignored this and kept punching.

Cold steel pressed against my temple. "Stay still or I'll blow your fucking head off."

It was then that I knew the rules of the streets had changed, and that if I survived this, then I would change too.

7

NEW BEGINNINGS

IT WAS ABOUT 2:30 AM when we arrived back at the apartment to split the proceeds from that evening's fruitful endeavor.

It was risky for me to stay behind and be the last person out, but I couldn't trust anyone else to take care of the loose ends. It was up to me to secure our exit. I jumped into the Nissan with Demus and drove around the block twice. Nothing seemed out of place or suspicious around the apartment, so he and I drove back to our place, performing the same check to make sure nothing was amiss.

Seeing the coast was clear, I hopped out of the car while we were still behind the building and half-jogged around to the front entrance. Tasha was just coming out, and instantly lit up as I approached. "Jimmy, what's up? You ever gonna take me home with you?"

"Of course. But right now, there's some heavy stuff on my plate. The minute that things settle down, and my relationship stagnates, I'll take you home. You can count on that."

"I hope so," she giggled. "I wanna see what all the fuss is about."

I leered at her for a moment, then smiled. "Anything I need to know?"

"Still nothing. Had my eyes open all night. Your buddies already got back. I didn't see them come in, but I know they're up there."

I nodded. "Listen for me when I come back down."

She looked confused.

"When I come back," I said, "follow me to my car. I got something for you."

I made my way up to the apartment where my crew was settling. I knocked twice, paused, then slapped the door with the palm of my hand. Screw opened the door.

"Bout time," he said. "We thought you might have ran into some problems on your way over."

"I epitomize caution," I replied. "Believe me when I tell you, if I had run into any problems, I'd have waited till it was safe before I came." I looked around. "Now what do we have?"

"Everything is ready and sorted," Scully explained as we walked toward the kitchen table where everything from the take sat. "I think we did alright. Not what I expected from the tip I had, but Nevil may have told the truth about moving the money. I don't think you'll be disappointed though."

"Okay," I said. "Let's get this done with."

I checked the table. "What we wind up with?"

NicNic stepped over and started pointing at things like he was Vanna White. "We got $45,000 in cash, four pounds, and two bricks of coke."

It wasn't as much as I was expecting from what Scully had told me, but I knew he expected more too.

I nodded. "We all know the breakdown. I'm gonna give Demus something out of my cut. We know he did good. But I also know none of you don't wanna part with one red cent of your own cut."

"Come on, Jimmy," Screw remarked, "you know I'll give him something outta mine. We couldn't have gotten anywhere without his driving."

I looked at everyone there, knowing they were not going to like what I was about to say. They knew the deal, and they knew how I operated, but I could tell they were going to bitch.

"You all take the drugs," I said. "Split all that between you all. Let me take 25 of the 45, and then you split the rest of the cash."

"That sounds like a decent offer," Alley started, "To you. But not to us. No disrespect," he continued, with a hint of nervousness and a bit of balls, "but in that deal, you get more than half the money, and leave us having to do all the work to get rid of the drugs. You know that shit has no value to us until we turn it into cash. So here we are, stuck with it while your part's done."

Calmly, I looked around the table, trying to gauge the faces of everyone sitting there. I wasn't going to spend a long period of time arguing my case. They either understood or they didn't.

"Okay." I focused on Alley. "I understand how you feel. I get that. But you do recall there have been many times when I have taken less, even though I had the right to a much bigger portion, right? I don't recall anyone else doing that."

I let that sit for a moment. Mainly because I wanted to see if anyone was going to challenge me on this. No one did. But as I waited for a response, the germ of an idea began to form in my head. Something potentially bigger and better. Something that now almost hinged on these guys not giving in. I gave it another few seconds to see if anyone would talk. When they didn't I broke the room's silence.

"You know what," I blurted out, "I'll take the drugs and you all keep the cash. I'll handle the risk of getting rid of this shit."

They were in shock, the statement throwing them for a loop. But this was only step one. This new plan of mine required them to not interfere with what I said. It required them to let me walk out with the drugs.

I could tell it was beginning to dawn on the smarter ones-- Screw, and maybe Alley--that I might have another play in mind. As far as they all knew, I'd always been consistent in my desire not to deal with drugs, and to just take cash. I hated handling drugs, and wanted nothing to do with them.

In most circumstances when it came to dealing with stolen drugs, the seller would need to take pennies on the dollar just to get rid of it. Plus all of the risk of actually selling the drugs-- from the cops and the people they were stolen from. They were beginning to wonder if I knew something they didn't, but they were also relieved that the cash would be theirs with no extra work involved.

NicNic finally broke the silence. "We gonna do jus' dat, bredrin. Gwann tek weh you a tek and we deal wid the rest of the money between us."

I nodded to Demus.

Shaking his head, he put the bundles of drugs into a bag, then walked out.

I spent another few moments looking at the guys around the table, conflicted. I liked this group. We'd worked well together, but this turn of events meant that we were done. They essentially turned on me for $45,000 when we could have made much more.

If the circumstances were different, I'd have been more annoyed at the situation. But I had a plan. And in order for it to work, I needed to leave these guys behind.

"I respect the choice," I said as I rose from the table, "but respect mine. We all can't work together anymore."

I walked out the door. Before I closed it, I turned back--I do have a heart--and told Screw that I'd link him. He nodded.

I let the door close behind me then walked down the stairs two at a time. When I got to the bottom, Tasha was standing there, waiting for me. We went to the car together. Demus was already sitting in the back seat.

He was a good guy.

I brought him on the job in case things went sideways. Demus was my safety net. He always had my back, and would always look out for me. In any kind of situation, he'd do what I asked him to do. He was loyal. And there were times when it seemed like he could read my mind. Like upstairs. He just knew that I had something else cooking, and understood that there was no use in complaining or trying to change things. He rolled with the punches and made sure I always came out on top.

Tasha, on the other hand, was bug-eyed as I opened the car door for her.

"What are you waiting for?" I asked. "I told you I had something for you. Get in and let me show you."

She was in disbelief. I'm pretty sure that she was thinking she'd never have the opportunity to get into a car with me, but here it was. We both got in, then I started the car and off we went.

While driving, Tasha stared out the window, either trying to figure out how to get back home, or looking with awe as we headed somewhere together.

I chuckled. "You're fine. We'll be there in a minute."

She showed me a bright smile.

If she was afraid at all, it was because of my reputation. But what I saw in that smile was pure happiness. She seemed glad to be in the car with me, almost like she'd won a prize.

I had no intentions other than business at that moment. I had Inez. I wasn't looking for someone on the side. I knew Tasha was interested--I'd have had to be the world's biggest idiot not to notice--but I wasn't when I asked her to get into the car.

That smile though.

There was something intoxicating about it. She was cute, that's for sure. And she was sweet and interesting. And loyal.

So was I.

I wasn't planning to do something to Inez I'd regret, even though I already did by bringing her into my way of living. But even I found myself feeling a little happy thanks to Tasha's infectious joy. I'd always known that Tasha would do whatever I'd ask, but this car ride gave me the understanding that there was something more to it. It was more than her trying to secure herself on the streets. It was more than just trying to use her closeness to me to get ahead. It was something else. But, I couldn't quite figure it out.

We stopped in front of an apartment building and Demus immediately jumped out and headed inside. I sat and waited a few minutes, until my beeper went off. I looked and saw Demus's code that everything was okay inside.

I turned to Tasha. "You've got a decision to make."

She looked at me wide-eyed.

"I've got an apartment in this building. I want you to stay here and keep an eye on it for me. It'll essentially be yours. You'll have the run of the place, and I'll come by periodically to make sure everything is taken care of. The bills are gonna get paid, but the decision is this: if you agree to stay here and look after things, you can't leave out. And you can't tell people where you're staying."

"But you'll be staying here sometimes too?" It was defi-nitely flirty, the way she asked, but it was also about comfort and protection.

"Yes," I answered. "This is my safe house. My safe haven, my refuge. It's why it's out here in the middle of nowhere. This is where I come when I need to lay low, relax, and unwind. Get away from things. But this is also why, Tasha," I stressed, "you cannot let anyone know where you're staying."

"Jimmy," she said, looking dead in my eyes, "you know I'd do anything for you."

I nodded.

Coyly, she asked, "You said you had something for me. Is it inside?"

"Tasha, sweetie," I leaned closer to her. "What I have for you is me. You're now a part of my life. That's what I've got for you. This is gonna change your life for the good."

We got out of the car and headed inside.

The apartment was modest. It wasn't too large--a good-sized living room where Demus parked himself on a couch, a den, a kitchen big enough for four, two bedrooms and one and a half bathrooms. The rooms had enough space for people to be comfortable, and if there were a large group in the apart-ment, it would easily accommodate them. The den had a few pieces of workout equipment, in addition to some comfortable chairs for a smaller and more intimate setting than the living room.

Tasha first walked into the bathroom and looked around before checking out the bedrooms. She seemed impressed, which was enough for me to know that she would enjoy spending her time in the apartment. I was waiting for her in the kitchen. When she finally walked in, she went straight for the fridge.

It was well-stocked with food items and some alcohol.

"You can always get the food you like later in the day," I said. "And we can get you some clothes."

She was like a deer in headlights, not quite sure of what to do.

"For right now," I continued, "if you want to change, there's some of my clothes in the bedroom closet. Put on a shirt or whatever."

She nodded and walked back into one of the bedrooms.

Demus rose off the couch. "That plan we discussed is a go?"

"Yeah," I said. "I'll link you later, but make sure the product gets to where we said it needs to be before you drop off the Nissan."

He gave me a *I know* look, but I ignored it. From most other guys, I'd have responded in a not-so-kind fashion. There's a level of respect I expect from the people that I work with.

Demus was an exception.

I'd known him a long time and I knew that there was little he wouldn't do for me. But I also knew that he was smart. We were often on the same page, instantly. Because of that, I gave him a bit of leeway. He was never disrespectful, but on occasion, there were those small reactions. I could get things done without Demus, but I sure as shit didn't want to.

I sat down in a chair as Demus walked out. I'd broken ties with some good guys, but it was for the best. They were self-interested and regularly mismanaged their money. That kind of behavior was going to leave us in a bad spot if we continued to operate that way. At this point, it was all just a liability.

It was only 4:30 AM, but I was dead tired. It had been a long night, and I just wanted to lay back and relax, catch a few Zs. I needed a shower first, but I could hear it running already. Tasha was taking one herself. I couldn't blame her--she had a long night too.

When she was done showering, I couldn't bring myself to get up yet. I was dog-tired and comfortable in the chair. Eventually, Tasha came back into the living room wearing one of my white Polo shirts. She sat down on the couch opposite me, hair wrapped in a bun. "I thought you'd be gone by now."

"I had plans to leave," I replied, "but sometimes there are reasons to stay. I need a night away to think through some things."

"Won't your woman be wondering where you're at?"

"My woman knows nothing about what I do, but she's smart enough to not ask questions about it either. If I'm away, I'm away. Sometimes I feel like I've corrupted her just by being with her."

"I don't think--"

"She's a good girl. I probably did corrupt her. But she's only gonna think I'm taking care of business." I sighed. "Look, let's just keep the conversation about her to a minimum, okay?"

Tasha smiled. "I guess that's probably best."

We sat there in the living room, not talking, for a few more minutes, and then I excused myself to take a shower.

As I stood under the water, I let the stresses of the day wash off. I reflected on everything that happened, and reassured myself that the decisions made were for the best. I don't often second-guess myself, but there are moments when I wonder if I may have acted prematurely. This was one of those times. I'd made a lot of big decisions in a small span of time. But they were carefully thought through, and I made the best decision I could at the time. The deal that I was trying to set up, and everything else that would come from it, would be something I'd need to deal with in the future. I had an idea of how things would play out, but until the gears started turning, everything was speculation.

I could have stood under the shower's spray for another

hour, just thinking about what might be, but I needed to get some sleep.

I toweled off, threw on a pair of boxer briefs and a tank top, and walked into the bedroom. I was tired and hungry as hell. The hunger could wait though. Sleep was needed--at least a few hours. I could operate perfectly well on only three hours of sleep a night. I'm one of those people who can get by with whatever I get, and run for weeks at a time off of that. There was something about spending that much time unconscious, unaware of my surroundings, not on guard, that bothered me. Asleep, I was subject to other people's whims. I never let myself get into a situation, or fall asleep somewhere, where I wasn't able to quickly defend myself. It was a concern always in the back of my mind.

Today's worry, however, was related to the plan I put in place. I wanted to remain awake so that I could think things through from every perceivable angle. I knew I never would-- there were always unexpected events and occurrences--but I'd try my best to see them all beforehand.

I slept longer than I wanted, waking up at 10:30. But with my body and mind fully recuperated, I felt ready for action. I would've slept longer, but I felt a presence, and instinctively grabbed my .44 Llama under my pillow.

I turned, pointed the gun at the presence, but it was only Tasha. Immediately, I lowered the gun.

She looked scared.

"Next time," I slipped the gun back under the pillow, "knock before walking in."

She nodded, but still seemed concerned.

"Come over here," I said, patting the bed. "What's wrong?"

She hesitated, then finally took the plunge and climbed in.

As she sat on the bed, legs crossed, I got my first really good look at her. I'd seen her before, definitely, but never in this way.

Never so casually, so calm, or in so little clothes. It was like I was seeing her for the first time. She had a sinuous mouth which enhanced her innocent green eyes. My shirt fit her so well, hugging her body in a way that looked exceptionally good.

"Jimmy," she said, hesitantly, "I've pretty much always been on my own. There's been other people in my life, but none of them ever really cared for me. Most of them were just trying to get at something."

She looked between her legs.

I understood her meaning. "I'm not--"

"*Shhhhh,*" she said. "That's the only thing I have that's really and truly my own. You understand? I'm not ready to part with it, and I'm not just gonna give it out willy nilly to anyone who's nice to me."

"I understand," I said. "In life, there's always gonna be a struggle, but the important thing about struggling is that it allows us to see ourselves in a way that we have never seen before, and it gives us that defining moment, when we're able to make a life-altering decision and change our situations. Point is, Tasha, you don't need to feel like it's a struggle here, or with me. I wanna help you out. You're a good girl. Let's just leave it there for now."

She smiled, then jumped out of bed.

"I'm gonna make you some eggs," she said while leaving the bedroom.

I continued to lay in bed, thinking about this new risk I'd assumed last night. I came a long way in my life not trusting anyone. But here I was, trusting Tasha.

What made her so special?

I trusted my gut, and my gut told me that I could rely on Tasha. That I should bring her into the fold. My gut had never steered me wrong, and I had no intention of questioning it now, but this brief pause made me wonder: of all the people in my life, everyone I could have placed my trust in, what made me pick Tasha?

I was broken out of this reverie when my beeper went off. It was the emergency code from my friend Nicole.

There were very few reasons Nicole would page me, especially with her emergency code.

I poked my head out the bedroom and heard Tasha making noise in the kitchen. Once the door was closed, I walked over to one of two phones I kept on my bedside table. The one I grabbed was there just to make outside calls, but it would not allow incoming calls. I dialed Nicole's number. After two rings, she answered. "I called Inez and she said she hasn't seen you in two days."

"Nicole, I know that's not what you paged me about. You know I don't discuss personal business. What'd you really link me for?"

She laughed on the other end of the phone call. "He said he'll meet with you, at a place of his choosing."

The ball was rolling.

"Where?"

"The Caribbean Beat," Nicole said. Big doings Friday night; everyone wild will be there."

"Not me," I said. "You know I don't do clubs."

"You will, if you want to do business with him. It's there, or nowhere."

"Are those his exact words?"

"Yeah," she said.

"Fine." I hung up.

Damn, I thought.

I've got less than twenty-four hours to get all this put in place. It was smart of him to arrange it so quickly. It didn't give me a chance to make any real arrangements. I didn't like to improvise, but I was usually good at it.

I heard noise outside the door, walked over, and opened it.

Tasha was standing outside, but she wasn't holding a plate of eggs.

"I didn't hear anything," she immediately said.

"Were you trying to?"

"No."

I sized her up and down as she stood there, coyly. I believed her. She seemed completely sincere.

As I continued to look at her, I was once again struck by her beauty. I reached out and gently put my hand on the back of her thigh, just below her ass. She didn't move.

I knew she wouldn't refuse me if I told her to get back into the bed, but that's not how I wanted it to happen. I wanted things to happen on her terms, when she was ready. I didn't want to be another guy who took something from her. I didn't want to be one of the many who she thought was just after her for one thing. I wanted her to understand that if that was going to happen, it was entirely up to her.

I understood patience.

Which is also why I wasn't anxious about the meeting I had with the guy they called Bull.

8

———————

ASSOCIATES

I SAT AT A BAR, observing everyone who entered. It was a Saturday night, the atmosphere inside was mellow, and the people inside were having a good time. I did my best not to draw unwanted attention, but every now and again, I could feel the eyes of some good looking girl on me.

I almost never went to nightclubs, but with one exception: if I was meeting someone for business. This was the place Bull wanted to meet, so I was obliged to come.

One of the DJs in the club I had connections with got me in early, avoiding the front door, the crowds, the cover charge, and the notoriety of swimming through the sea of people waiting to get in. This allowed me to bring my gun inside, affording me a sense of security at this meeting.

I'd heard about Bull. I'd known his reputation. I had some mutual acquaintances with him, but I didn't know him. Never met him. I wanted to make sure that I felt safe at this meeting.

Though, I didn't expect anything would happen.

I generally carried myself in this way. You never knew what kind of trouble you might run into in various situations, so I strongly believed it was important to be prepared for all eventualities.

Clubs were notorious for mistakes being made. There was so much to distract you, so much to take your focus away from the deal or alliance you were trying to make. I made it my business to remain focused at all times while in a club. The music, lights, girls, none of that was going to distract me from business.

It was life or death. I'm generally a well-liked guy--at least I think I am--but I've made some enemies over the years. And a place like this is the perfect spot to take care of someone you don't like. Large crowds, the potential for lots of confusion. If I was going to take out an enemy and wanted there to be complete chaos after, I'd probably pick a nightclub. So I stayed on guard when visiting places like this.

After an hour went by, more people started filing into the club. I became more vigilant. I was discreet in my observations of people coming and going. I paid little to no attention to flirtatious women or anyone trying to make conversation with me. I was laser-focused.

That's when I spotted Demus walking with Bull in tow. They both immediately headed in my direction. On occasion, Demus would stop to say hello to someone or whisper into the ear of a gorgeous woman as he progressed through the throngs of people.

Humored by his attempts to make some moves, I chuckled. Demus could be a real character. He was always able to seamlessly integrate himself into whatever environment he was in, staying cool, calm, and collected as he walked through the crowd. But I could tell he was laser-focused on pressing on and getting to me. When Demus finally did, he and Bull each sat on a stool.

Bull was well-dressed, sitting in a comfortable silk shirt and a pair of slacks, a diamond chain on his neck that matched his bracelet and middle finger ring.

Demus ordered a Heineken for himself and a Guiness Stout for Bull. I don't generally drink. Not really my thing. But if I do, while I have no real problems enjoying a beer, it is almost always Jamaican 100% overproof white rum for me. For that reason, I declined Demus's offer of a beer, and waited for the vibes among the three of us to feel right.

I was about to say something to Demus, indicating for him to go do something else so that Bull and I could get down to business, but he already read my mind. Demus got up and headed off to another corner of the club. Bull and I nodded at each other.

It was time to get down to business.

"So you're the elusive Jimmy," Bull said. "The fella everyone talks about, but few get to see."

"I'd consider that an asset," I responded. "Don't you think? Especially for someone with the reputation I've got."

"That depends on one's profession, I'd suppose."

We both shared a small chuckle and took a sip of our respective drinks.

"But," he continued, "we're not here to discuss that, are we?"

"Of course not." I looked around to see if anyone was within earshot, but there didn't seem to be.

"I'm sure Demus spoke with you about what my plans are," I stated. "Before I go into details though, I need to know you're going to be able to meet the demands I have for the product."

Bull flashed an appreciative smile at me. He struck me as the type that respected a no bullshit approach to things. A real businessman. As a rule, I don't feed people lines of bullshit anyway, but I can if the situation calls for it.

"I can meet your demands," Bull said, "but are you sure

that you will be able to do exactly what you're setting out to do? I can think of several people that will be exceptionally unhappy with you making those kinds of moves."

I shrugged.

"Look," he sighed, "I know people fear you. You've got a reputation, and there are plenty who know what you're about. However, there are those who are willing to go to war over that kind of money."

"You let me deal with all that, and just focus on getting that delivered where and when I need it."

He nodded, stood up, and made his move to leave. As he brushed by me, he leaned down and said, "Understand you only get one mistake with me. In this business there is no room for error. I would strongly advise you to change how you're moving. Image is everything. The one you have now is completely unnecessary in my line of work."

He continued on his way without looking back, blending in with the crowd.

Demus was back at my side before I even realized it. "Looked like that went well."

"I won't know for sure until we're conducting business regularly, but I think it did. I can assure you though, my friend, our lives are about to change."

***

DRIVING BACK TO THE APARTMENT, I kept thinking about the conversation that I had with my soon-to-be business partner. I didn't know much about him. I knew that he went by Bull and was a major player in the drug game. There were a lot of rumors and speculation about how he rose to the top, and how he got to be so powerful, but I ignored all of that and focused only on the facts that were known to me. These facts tended to add up.

From what I knew from my connects in the street, he was a generally good dude, a stand-up fellow, someone who could be trusted. Personally, I didn't care for how he flaunted his success, but I knew that in the grand scheme of things, it wouldn't affect how we would do business together, so I didn't let it bother me.

It was late when I got back to the apartment and parked the car.

I figured that I'd head upstairs and pass out, maybe eat something, but when I opened the door, Tasha was sitting on the sofa watching TV.

She had something different on from what she was wearing earlier that evening. After looking at it, I realized that she had nothing like that, at all, in the apartment.

I walked past her and into the bedroom and sat down on the edge of the bed, contemplating my next move. This would be crucial. If I were to be successful with this plan, I needed to be careful and think things through, consider any possible collateral damage that might be caused. I was pretty confident that everything would work out as I expected, but you could never be sure in any endeavor.

I hadn't been home in two days. Inez would be wondering where I was. She wouldn't worry, she knew I would do things like this on occasion, but she would want to Know when I'd be back.

While thinking about Inez, I realized that I needed to be done with that chapter of my life. It wasn't that I didn't love her. It was the fact that she was a good girl. She was innocent. She didn't deserve to be dragged down by the things I was doing, or the things I had done. It would be better for both of us if I were to just move on. I didn't want to ruin her life. She deserved better.

I knew she would tell me it was her decision to make.

Maybe it was. But in this moment, I was going to be selfish and make the decision for her. Much as she might not agree, it was the right decision. Things were about to get a lot more dangerous, and she needed to be far away from that.

Tasha, on the other hand, would be able to hold her own. She knew the street code and how to handle herself. I had little to worry about if Tasha got involved in my work. She was loyal, strong, and smart. She could get through most situations, and I wouldn't need to worry about ruining her.

My train of thought was broken by my rumbling gut. It felt like my stomach was touching my back. I'd eaten nothing all night, and the alcohol wasn't helping matters.

I took myself into the kitchen and started looking through the fridge to find something to eat. As I examined the cold cuts and other stuff in there, I heard bubbling coming from the stove. Intrigued, I glanced up and noticed a pot sitting on the stovetop.

"Tasha," I called, "what's bubbling in the pot?"

"I figured you didn't eat while you were out," she replied, "so I made some stew peas with rice and some fish on the side." Tasha walked into the kitchen and stirred the contents of the pot. "That's all you. I ate earlier."

I looked at her confused. I appreciate someone taking the time to take care of me, but I wasn't expecting it from Tasha. I reached up to one of the cabinets and grabbed a bowl.

Tasha, just as quickly, took the bowl from my hands and started spooning some rice into it. "I also threw out all of those nasty looking container meals in the fridge. They looked terrible." She set the bowl of rice down on the counter and put some fish over top of it. "Tomorrow, I'll run to a store and get some stuff that I can cook. You'll like it better than any of that."

I felt transfixed as I watched her prepare my plate. I didn't know what to make of this. I'd known Tasha for a while, but I didn't know her to be so forceful. Not that it was a bad look on her. She just always came off as more submissive, demure. But I could learn to like this new Tasha.

Before she could do it for me, I grabbed a fork out of the utensil drawer and took a bite of the rice and fish. It was incredible.

"While you were out," Tasha went on, "I went back to where I was staying and grabbed some stuff I couldn't part with. I also grabbed some of the cash you left behind to get the ingredients for this. I hope you don't mind?"

"'Mind,'" I said. "I definitely don't mind. This is a smash hit. Some of the best I ever had."

I carried the bowl into the living room and continued to eat on the sofa, trying to keep myself awake as a wave of exhaustion swept over me.

Tasha sat with me. She wasn't awkwardly staring at me, watching me eat. But neither was she weirdly staring at one of the walls. It almost felt like we were a long-established couple just relaxing together on the sofa after a long day at work.

When I was finished, Tasha took the bowl from me.

"I'm going to clean up," she said. "Why don't you jump in the shower? Go get refreshed."

I nodded and we separated; she went to the kitchen and I walked into the bedroom. Before taking a shower, I needed to make a quick call to my associates, let them know that every-thing was in motion and ready to move.

The call didn't take long, and I knew that the word would spread to the people that needed to know. Finally feeling relaxed, with no more business to take care of, I got undressed and stepped into the shower.

I let the water run colder than normal, but I'd always found cold showers more relaxing. I stood under the spray for a few minutes, washed up, then stood under it for a little while longer.

As I walked back into the bedroom, I heard Tasha still in the kitchen cleaning up. It made me smile thinking about how comfortable she felt. And how comfortable I felt.

I flopped down on the bed and laid back, drifting off to sleep. Next thing I knew, I felt someone crawling into the bed next to me. I didn't need to reach for my gun this time around.

"What's up, Tasha?"

"Nothin'." She coyly looked over at me.

"You wanna kick it for a little bit? I was gonna smoke some anyway."

Her eyes lit up as she smiled and reached over to the night-stand, grabbing a backwood and some weed. I watched closely as she rolled the blunt tight and licked the leaf to seal it.

"Jimmy," she hesitated, "I want to thank you for letting me stay with you, but I can't help but think there's a bigger reason for me to be here."

"There is. I'm not gonna lie. I gotta put some things together and in motion, and you're gonna hold down some stuff for me, but think of this as your place. It kinda is. I'm gonna take care of you for doing some important things for me. And I'll be here off and on. But you can't let anyone know what you're doing."

She nodded.

I took the blunt from her and lit it, enjoying a long drag. I passed it to her and she took a hit. We smoked in silence, just enjoying the company and weed. As we finished up, I gave her a serious look. "Do you have anything that I need to know about?"

Tasha shook her head.

"Is there anything you need to make you more comfortable here?" I asked. "I want you to be comfortable because I need your absolute, complete commitment. Are there any loose ends that need to be tied up? Any distractions that need to be gotten rid of? Anything that might get in the way of me having your undivided attention?"

"No Jimmy. My life isn't that complicated. I'll be here for whatever you need."

"Okay. Cause there's no going back now."

She saw the seriousness in my eyes and nodded.

Now that business had been taken care of, we both laid back.

I appreciated that she reacted to the weed in the same way that I do. It doesn't make me eat or giggle or paranoid or anything like that. It just mellows me. It did the same for her.

I laid there, looking at her, thinking about everything that I'd started. I was content.

She shook me out of my thoughts when she slid down to the end of the bed, stood up, and let her nightgown slip to the floor. It was like it was happening in slow motion. The gown fell, slowly, and underneath it all she had on was a pair of silk panties. I couldn't believe the body she had.

I'd known Tasha for years. She usually wore something that hid her body rather than show it off. I expected she had a killer body, but I was totally unprepared for what I saw standing before me.

Seeing my surprise, she smiled appreciatively, looking completely satisfied by the compliment. She crawled back into the bed and rested her head on my chest. Looked up into my eyes. There was an innocence in her gaze, but also something else. Something fierce. Something animalistic. She was just waiting for something.

"Are you sure you want this?" I asked.

"If you want me."

That was all I needed.

I turned, pulled her mouth to mine, and kissed her deeply.

There had been a sexual tension building between us for years. Despite the fact that Tasha barely showed off, and despite the fact that I never really gave her more than a passing glance, the sex we were about to have was as unpreventable as the rising morning sun rising.

This was fate. This was kismet. This was inevitable.

I rolled Tasha onto her back and slowly moved down the bed, planting kisses along her body. As I reached her panties, I slowly pulled them off over curves that I never even knew she could possess. I threw them to the floor, and then went back up, leaving another trail of kisses until I reached her breasts. I circled each nipple, spending minutes caressing them with my mouth until they were stiff, and then flicked my tongue over them. They were swollen and turgid. When I blew air on them, Tasha shuddered, eyes rolling back as she arched her back.

She was in heaven.

Slowly, I spread Tasha's legs with my knees, worked my way up from the nipples to her lips. Then her ear lobe, nibbling on them for a moment.

I whispered in her ear. "Take it in your hands."

She did.

"Just like that. Slide it up and down between your lips."

She followed instructions.

As Tasha worked it between her lips, I went back to her breasts, caressing and exploring every inch of them. But after a little while, I could tell that we were both just waiting for what was coming. I moved my hands around to Tasha's back and then down to her cheeks. I spread them wide and lifted them. I could feel her tensing with anticipation of the penetration that was about to happen.

She gasped as I slid inside her, gyrating her hips as we moved in sync. I pushed forward, she moaned. We continued at a slow pace for a few minutes, getting a feel for each other.

I thrusted. She sucked in a deep breath.

I took it up a notch, pulling almost all of the way out and then thrusting back in. I felt Tasha's muscles spasming with her orgasms, and I could see the ecstasy written on her face. She was enjoying every second of it. Tasha looked up at me with tears of joy and a huge, content smile on her face.

I wasn't ready to be done, and Tasha seemed like she could keep going and coming. I leaned in and kissed her everywhere: her face, her lips, her eyes, her cheeks, all while maintaining the pace.

I wanted to come with her. I wanted her to feel my climax as she felt her own. I wanted her to feel the fullness of both of us completely satisfied.

We were sweaty and slick, but we were both beyond elation. Tasha was close to something massive. I continued to thrust, letting her just lay back and enjoy as I was building up to something huge as well.

I slid almost all the way out and slowly pushed back in.

I did this once.

Twice.

Three more times.

We both were anticipating the release, but dreading the separation that comes with the end. The time was nearly there, so I pulled out, leaving the scantest bit of the head inside, and slowly pushed back in as far as I could. Tasha screamed as her orgasm hit. Then it turned into a deep, guttural moan. I released at the same time, moaning in pleasure as I fell to her side, both of us panting, sweaty, and in bliss.

9

RETURNED

NIGHTTIME FOUND me where it normally does: wide awake, preparing myself to go out and get something done. I inhabited this nocturnal world. It was where I was most in my element.

It was my world.

The world of the sun, with bright lights and businessmen running in and out of buildings, was as far from my own reality as you could get. So, as usual, I jumped in the shower for the first time of the day after the sun had gone down.

I didn't spend the earlier part of the day in bed though.

Tasha left the apartment around noon to run some errands and get some supplies for my newest endeavor. Demus stopped by with the leftovers from the robbery to stash them. This was the largest amount of foot traffic that I'd have liked at the apartment, but we kept it to the absolute minimum by making it a rule not to have many people coming and going. On rare occasions, we'd have one or two people there for business. We allowed for no disturbances or problems. As far as our neighbors were concerned, we were the best possible people: quiet, courteous, and friendly.

When Demus stopped by at 4:30 AM with the leftover product, he smiled at the neighbors and said hello. They may not have known him by name, but they had seen him enough to know he belonged in the building.

I marveled at the fact Demus seemed like he never slept. I kept strange hours, but with Demus, no matter when I called him, he sounded like he was wide awake and ready to go.

I got out of the shower and threw on all black clothes before calling some of the guys I was about to deal with, making plans to meet at the little Jamaican store we frequented. I knew the owner, Dor, so it was a perfect place to meet. We ate well whenever there, and since she kept quiet about our discussions and activity, we always left a big tip to show our appreciation for her discretion.

After grabbing some money and my keys, I headed out the door into the night.

I liked to take the back way out and circle the block to make sure everything was on the up-and-up. I was feeling good as I got into the car and threw a cassette of Studio One music into the player. As the tape played, Peter Tosh came out of the car's speakers, and I was in heaven. When it comes to reggae, Bob Marley is great--there is absolutely no doubt about that--but I'll take Peter Tosh over him any day. Tosh's struggles were real. I loved how he fought the system, the same system that always abused and oppressed us as a people, and how he tried in so many different ways to keep us from stagnating, from being illiterate, which is precisely what those oppressors wanted.

As I drove, I thought about the bold move I was about to make. How everything would play out right. I had planned well and thought things through enough, but success was just one of many options, and the best laid plans of mice and men often go awry. After all, God laughs in the face of mans' plans. Despite these thoughts, I remained positive. I believed this plan was going to work.

The only catch that I could truly envision was the aftermath of the lick that got us the product. We robbed the coke from some serious guys who would have no trouble retaliating if they discovered who robbed them. Fortunately, I knew that I covered my tracks. I just wasn't completely sure about my compatriots. It was possible one of them slipped or did something stupid that caused a tiny clue to be left behind. They weren't dumb, but they had a tendency to act like complete nincompoops. If they did, their blunder could work their way back to me.

I severed ties with them though, and likely did it in a timely enough fashion to keep anything from blowing back on me.

Shaking these thoughts out of my head for the moment, I let myself enjoy the music as I finished the drive. I had about ten minutes before I'd get to the Jamaican spot. It was time to focus. I needed to be on my game. These were guys who took their business seriously. I needed to make a good first impression in order for them to understand that if we were going in business together, we all needed to have each others' backs.

By the time I arrived, three of the guys were already there, parking their cars out front of the Jamaican spot as I turned onto Park Avenue. I circled the block, looking for a parking space around the corner, preferably in the cut so that I could walk to the store without drawing too much attention. Once finding a decent spot, I made my way to the back entrance of the store, knocked twice, then let myself in. I was greeted by the cooks and workers who'd known me for years. They were always happy to see me, and every time I came in, there were cheers of merriment as I made my way around, greeting everyone like they were family.

As I did this, I noticed that Demus was already there, and had stationed himself in the kitchen to wait for my arrival.

"Hey, Jimmy," he said, standing to greet me.

"What's goin' on?" I wanted information about the guys we were meeting.

Demus explained the situation.

We both knew these guys, but not in any significant way. They were all sort of loners. Demus had spent some time talking to them, however, and had learned a little more. "They all have potential to be good. They just need someone to direct them and help them get over their egos. They're all on this big-me-little-you kind of nonsense."

I glanced out the kitchen door window and saw them sitting around munching on Jamaican beef patties with some Kola Champagne to wash it down. They looked exactly as Demus described. None of them was talking to any of the others.

"They need to get rid of their pride," Demus continued. "They were reluctant to link up. They all spent a lot of time only looking out for themselves."

I knew that when we first got in touch with these guys.

It wasn't surprising. If you're making money on your own, and you've got a good hustle, you really don't need anyone else. Linking up with someone else might be a liability, and in this line of work, those can be deadly.

Demus went on. "There are some issues that need to be addressed. Everyone is not in complete agreement with the plan. But they can be convinced."

"How much convincing?" I asked.

"Not a lot. None of them has their own plan. Right now, your plan is the best. They may be lone wolves, but they're looking for someone to point them in the right direction."

I thought about this for a second. "So it'll be easy for me to step in and help give them some direction?"

Demus nodded.

I looked through the window once more at the crew. It certainly wasn't perfect, but if they could be molded into something solid, then everything would be good. At this time though, there were so many crews vying for the top spot in the narcotics game. In order to dominate, you needed to do things that set you apart.

I believed violence was that thing.

Mind you, not indiscriminate violence, gratuitous violence, or violence just for violence's sake. No one survives or prospers when recklessness and chaos reign. But controlled violence--the kind that is used for a real purpose--that makes a crew stand out enough to rise up the food chain. Dealing out appropriate punishments for wrongdoings earned a person respect. Understanding when it was best to apply force gets you a reputation for being fair. Fairness, in turn, earns you a reputation as someone not to fuck with, and as someone who you could do business with.

Consider: you run a crew, but every time a business deal goes awry, you kill them. No one will want to do business with you, because they're utterly afraid.

Now consider: you run a crew, but every time someone messes up, you forgive them and hope they'll learn their lesson. Anyone who does business with you will step all over you and squish you underneath their shoe like the little bug you are.

But there's an alternative.

You run a crew. One of your guys fucks up royally. Another one makes a minor slip up. The first guy might land you in jail, the second might cost you a few dollars. You punish both, but in accordance with the severity of their misdeed. You demonstrate that you are fair by punishing those who don't recognize their mistake or the potential of one, and that, when crossed, you don't hesitate.

This is what I believe in.

Could I punish someone by beating them within an inch of their life? Of course. But would I do it for something that doesn't deserve that kind of punishment? Never.

Recklessness and chaos both have no place in this business, but correctly meted out violence does.

I don't like liabilities, which is why I generally do things on my own. I assumed all the risk without leaving anything to chance. If I controlled everything, no one could drag me down. But in this circumstance, my decision to bring these guys in on this plan was well thought out. I wasn't going to make this my life-long career, but I also didn't intend on making a prison cell my retirement plan. I knew that I needed to utilize caution with every step I took, especially with these guys.

Which is why I already planned my way out if it came to that.

Nothing was going to connect me back to these guys. We would not socialize, we would not call each other regularly to discuss anything, we would not send Christmas or birthday cards, we would not let our women know each other or hang out. There would be no connections between us, except for the money that we would split for conducting solid business.

In the world I inhabited, men only came together for one of two things: to get money or go to war.

I stepped out into the restaurant, with Demus following, and greeted them all respectfully. I treated them as I wanted to be treated, followed the Golden Rule and all that. I wanted to make them all feel comfortable. I wanted them thinking we were all equals coming together, and that we all had something to bring to the table.

"Gentlemen," I said, "so wah really ah gwaan wid de mon dem?"

"You tell us wah gwaan," Demo said. "We're all here because you said dat we can all help each other make some money."

I nodded.

Demo continued. "I can't understand why we should link up as a crew. What you're proposing, we're already doing: making money. On our own. What is the financial advantage to linking up with you?"

He asked a valid question. And by looking around the table, I could tell that this was the chief concern of the others as well.

"The difference," I said, "is that we will be doing it in a more organized manner. The risk factor will diminish because of that. In short, we will continue to do this business and continue to make money, but we will be doing it from a position that assumes far less risk for each of us."

"Jimmy, everyone knows how you operate," Ozzie said. "We are all aware of the fact that you and your last crew fell out over some money business."

I expected something like this from Ozzie. He spoke intelligently, and often would not speak unless it was important for him to do so. His words meant more to the guys at the table than anyone else's. If I could sway him, the others would fall in line.

"You're not completely wrong," I responded, "but that's not the whole story. Some of it was money, some was something else that we don't need to get into. I don't make a habit of sharing other people's business or harping on it."

I paused and looked around the table. I wanted to see everyone's reactions. It was important to know if they were here just to gossip, or here to discuss business.

Their facial expressions told me that I could go on. I looked directly at Ozzie as I spoke. "Before you came here, I told you all what I'm about. I also told you that if you weren't interested, all you had to do was not show up. I'd have known your choice and there would be no hard feelings. But you're all here." At this, I stopped and looked at all three of them. "Because you all showed up, what this tells me is that you're all with it."

They all bobbled their heads. It wasn't quite a nod of agreement, but it did tell me that I had their attention.

"I'll admit that the ganja trade is good for you all," I said. "But it's good in bulk. And while that's true, you're not actually seeing the profit you want to be seeing, or the profit you want people to believe you have. I offer you a cheaper price and therefore a larger profit. Something real. You get a pretty penny for yourselves and get the life you want. No hassles and being in the fast lane."

Again, more head bobbles, but I was focused on Ozzie. It was him I was working to convince, and I could see that we were at least on the same page. I may have been a paragraph ahead of him, but the same page nonetheless.

"I've got the resources and the muscle to get us where we need to be," I told them all. "All I need to know from each of you is whether you're in or out."

Each one of them seemed nervous. They looked at each other as if trying to figure out if I wanted the answer right that second. To ease the tension, I stood up.

"Mi raw and ready fi nyam some food," I said. "I'm gonna go order some, spend a little time eating. When I come back, I want to know if you're all on board. We've got a bunch of resources we need to pool together if we're doing this, so we gotta get moving. Now, if you'll excuse me."

I walked to the counter to order my food. Out of the corner of my eye, I saw Ozzie coming up to me.

"I'm with you," he said. "I'm going to talk to the others when I link them later. I'll probably be able to get them all around to it. There's one I'm a little concerned about, but we could probably kick him loose and not worry."

"Okay," I said. "I'm counting on you, cause we need to get this up and running as soon as possible. We've already wasted enough time talking about it, you know?"

Changing the subject, Ozzie asked, "Is your connect who I think it is?"

" Ozzie, you know that loose lips sink ships. I can't and won't disclose anything until I know we're in business, so for the moment, it's important to remain discreet."

Ozzie nodded.

I turned to Dor and ordered my meal: butter fish and dumplings with an order of cod soup and cooked yams and bananas on the side.

Ozzie and I walked back to the table, content that a deal had been reached. Now that Ozzie was in, he'd be able to get everyone else to come around the plane.

The others got up to order their food as we sat down. When they returned with their curry chicken and oxtails, we all ate and talked about de gyal dem and other things.

After finishing my meal, I told them I had to run, and instructed Demus to take care of the owner with a generous tip like always.

I drove back to the apartment, circling the block a few times before parking to make sure all was good, then headed to the apartment to see if Tasha had taken care of what I'd asked her.

I was growing closer and closer to Tasha. The more time we spent together, the more I realized I was into her. I knew that it could be a problem. Not because it would distract me, but because it gave other people an in. It would be a potential weak spot. I didn't like that, but she was kind, caring, and passionate.

She also had a good head on her shoulders and I knew that I could count on her.

As I walked toward the apartment, I kept thinking that it was good fortune to have found her and get to know her a little bit. She was always helpful in other situations, and now, she seemed like a godsend. She took care of the things that I had little time to deal with on my own.

I was glad to have her in my life. It wasn't love or anything like that, certainly not yet, but I was glad to have her anyway.

10

BEEF

IT WAS A VERY warm evening in Brooklyn and the street was bustling. People acted like they were invincible at this hour, as if the night wouldn't keep moving along and leave them behind. People weren't themselves at night; they became someone new when the sun went down. Work clothes came off and the night time ensemble was put on. This transformed a person from the mundane person they were during business hours into someone remarkable.

But people feared the night.

Children were beckoned home before the streetlights came on. Cautious people hurried from buses and subways to get into their apartments before dark. These people weren't wrong to be afraid. Death lurked in the night. Around every corner, on the other side of a bodega, just beyond the bright touch of a streetlight, death wandered. For some, merely surviving the night was a feat in and of itself.

On the corner of Franklin Street and Lincoln, two men sat in a Toyota Cressida with smoke-tinted windows.

"Are you sure it was him?" Sprag asked, breaking the car's silence.

Scully gave him an incredulous look. "Yes, I'm sure."

"How sure?"

"Sure enough to know that it was $45,000, two keys of coke, and a shitload of weed. That's how sure."

"How you nuh dat? If mi find out seh yuh did dehpon it too, me ah goh brush you, don't play wid me."

Scully backed up. "I had nothing to do with it. But I know some very disgruntled men who would love to see him get his."

"Ahh, I see," Sprag said. "You want me to do something you are afraid to do on your own. You give me a little info that was-- what, supposed to wet my whistle? Get me interested? Go off and do your dirty work?"

Scully didn't know whether or not to nod.

Sprag went on. "You bring me this information, not just about some guy I can't stand, but about a guy who likely robbed me. Who left a permanent scar across my face. A man that I would absolutely love to see dead, lying on the street in a pool of his own blood. Mek mi tell you something, Scully, I think you know more than you're letting on. I think you know a lot more than you're willing to part with. We gonna talk again, but next time, you gonna be more forthcoming."

Scully paused. "Yeah..."

"Get the hell out my car."

The car stopped.

Scully opened the door, put one leg on the street, and no sooner did his other leg leave the car did Sprag pull away, reaching over to close the door on his own. Scully lost his balance and fell, rolling along the side of the car before landing on his ass in the middle of the street. He watched as Sprag made a U-turn and headed off in the opposite direction.

Scully knew his inflated ego was bruised, though it took him a second to realize that his side was too. He felt low. Dirty. But he didn't care. Sprag was soon going to remove a major pain Scully had longer than either of his new bruises. And it was worth it.

Fyngaz will soon be out of the picture, he thought. *And once that happens, I can slip into the vacuum created by his absence.*

"Fuck him," Scully mumbled, still sitting on the asphalt.

He pushed himself up, brushed off his pants' backside, and headed down the block toward his car. Once there, he got in, lit a spliff and turned the music up, loud. He laid back smoking as Buju Bonton a.k.a. Gargamel sang Man Fi Dead through the speakers of his car. Despite the music and the weed, he wasn't mellowing out. All he could think about was what had him so twisted to begin with: Fyngaz last words that night.

"Screw, I'll link you."

It was the biggest insult. We all can't work together anymore over some bullshit, but he'll still link Screw? What kind of bullshit was that?

"Motherfucker's gonna get his."

"LISTEN, INEZ," I said. "I understand how you feel. There's no defense that I can offer that's gonna soften this. Truth is, our relationship has been strained at best for a long time."

Glaring at me, Inez threw her hands up in frustration. When she opened her mouth to speak, I held up a hand.

"You remember when we first met, you said you didn't want to know nothing about what I do and didn't want to be involved in anything I did?"

She nodded.

"Well, things are getting too tight right now. There's too

much of a chance you're going to be involved. You're going to know more than you want to."

We were having this conversation in the car. I was in the front passenger seat and Inez was driving. Ozzie and Demus were in the back. It wasn't optimal, I didn't need them being a part of this conversation, but there was little I could do about that.

Circumstances led us here, and made this the time to hash things out. The universe didn't seem to mind that Demus and Ozzie were there with us. And neither did Inez.

It was the middle of the day. Out of character for me. Normally, I'm nocturnal. A vampire. But today, I was out and about while the sun shone. I wanted to show Ozzie a few spots in the area that he should know about, so we all decided to take a drive then find someplace to grab a bite.

Inez wanted to come. She was talking about wanting to be more a part of my life. That's what prompted this very conversation.

The whole point of this discussion, the whole reason I felt we needed to have this talk, was because I needed her to be less a part of my life. I needed to keep her away from all this. To take her out of his life. I needed to stay away to keep her safe.

I felt bad.

Inez was great. But I didn't want her ruined because she was with me. I didn't want her to be a target, or for someone to try and use her to get to me. I wanted her safe, out of the way. The only way was to end it before it was too late. Let her go off and find someone who walked the straight and narrow. I never wanted her to see the gritty side of life. She was too good, too pure. I wouldn't be able to explain all of that without telling her more about myself than she wanted to know.

"I respect you too much," I said. "I want what's best for you."

We were slowing down at an intersection as I explained this to her. Inez pulled into the turn lane to make a left. That was when I noticed a guy with his head down walking toward the car, hands tucked into his hoodie's pockets. He was making a bee-line for the car.

As I tried to make out who this guy was, there was an explosion to my right. The window next to me was obliterated. A shower of small glass fragments fell on my shoulder and arm and into my lap.

At that same moment, the guy in the hoodie pulled out a gun and started shooting at the windshield. It exploded into a million tiny pieces.

Time slowed down.

Demus jumped out.

Inez screamed.

I ducked. Pulled the lever on the driver's seat to make it fall all the way back and lay Inez horizontally. Turned to Ozzie. "Keep her safe."

I opened my door and jumped out to join Demus, who was already firing back with his 18-shot 9 Taurus. He never leaves home without it. There were four men in total. One was down on the ground. As I turned away from him and took aim at one of the shooters, I noticed him slowly rise to his feet. Out of pure instinct, I turned around and saw him hobbling down the street, away from the fracas.

Glass littered the street. Bystanders crowded the sidewalk. In the middle of everything was Demus, myself, and three other guys. I recognized one of them, and immediately knew who was behind this, but that didn't matter now. A few bullets were still flying as the three would-be assassins turned tail and ran off.

Demus chased after one as I hurried to the car.

I opened the driver's side door and pushed Inez over into

the passenger seat. Ozzie was still in the back. He wasn't cowering, but I could tell he was glad I gave him leave to stay in the car, protected.

I jumped inside, closed the bullet riddled door, and floored it, stopping only to let Demus jump into the back seat.

It looked bad.

Really bad.

It was a miracle none of us got hit. Especially Inez. I had more on my mind than the conversation we had only a few minutes ago, but as I looked at her, I could tell she finally understood what I had been talking about. Mentally checking that off my list, I was glad to know I could drop Inez off at home without having to worry about her, though it had significantly dropped in priority in light of everything that occurred. All the shit I needed to worry about weighed me down.

After bringing Inez home, Demus, Ozzie and I sat in a different car, talking. Demus recognized one of the shooters. He and I had the same idea of what needed to happen.

The guy who'd shot the front windshield--the one in the hoodie--was known as Jackie Chan. That told us everything we needed to know about who was really behind this. But the bigger question for us was how they had any idea where or when we'd be there.

Jackie Chan was a sudden itch that needed to be scratched. There was no time to let it cool and see if it would go away on its own. I had big fish in the fryer and no time to waste on stupid loose ends. Jackie Chan wasn't the loose end, but his presence there let me know exactly who was. I wasn't happy about it, but this meant I was taking a trip to East Orange.

A trip I needed to do alone.

I dropped off Demus and Ozzie then headed out.

Later that day, I found myself outside the building of my destination. I needed to make sure that I wouldn't be seen before, or after, I took care of this business. There didn't appear to be many eyes on the building, but I knew from my experiences that the fewer eyes there seemed to be on a particular place, the more there actually were.

I had to be stealthy. My best bet would be to enter from the back of the building. This was not a time for brazen acts. This was a moment for subtlety.

I knew who I was going to see. I knew how he acted. He most likely thought that he'd be untouchable, feeling secure in his home base, and that if someone were to come after him, it would be out on the street, in the open. He believed that, at home, he was invincible.

I was about to teach him a valuable lesson.

No one can perceive every eventuality. It isn't possible. But smart people consider broad strokes. I might not be able to envision every way someone might attack me in my home, but I could certainly imagine a scenario in which someone tried to. He, on the other hand, was so wrapped up in himself that he couldn't even picture someone hitting him where he lived.

He was too lax.

Sure, he had some small things in place, some little bits of insurance, but they weren't good enough.

Two young boys sat on the steps leading into the building. They were bouncing a ball, seemingly waiting for something. From my own childhood, I knew the best lookouts were kids like this. Little kids, even teenagers, were the best lookouts you could find since people generally overlooked them.

As I neared the door to the building, I grew cautious of these two kids. Were they his lookouts? Were they going to alert him that some stranger they'd never seen before was coming into the building? I certainly didn't look like a cop, so they weren't going to make that assumption, but I was unknown to them. Those were the two things they'd be told to look out for.

I had no choice. I had to risk letting them sound the alarm by being seen. It would be silly to abort at this point. I was here. There was already a chance they saw me.

I stopped for a moment as I heard the sound of the elevator doors open. Two women stepped out. The boys turned, saw the women, and jumped up to go meet them. The foursome then left the building through the front door.

I breathed a little easier. My luck was still holding. No one was acting as a lookout.

I entered the building, confidently strode to the elevator, walking through the doors as they began to close, and hit the button for the fifth floor. I couldn't be sure that he'd be alone in the apartment. I needed to blitz the place.

When the elevator opened, I went straight for the apartment door and put my ear against it. Listened. Nothing.

He could be alone.

He could be with someone, but neither of them were talking.

He could be with a dozen people in a back room and I just couldn't hear anything.

There were too many options. But I was here, ready to go, and I was not going to stop until I got to the bottom of things. I knocked on the door, then stepped to the side, out of the peephole's sight.

"What?" A muffled voice replied.

I didn't move.

Feet shuffled away from the door.

I knocked again. Louder and more forceful.

"Who the fuck is it?"

I didn't respond.

The feet shuffled away again. This time, I waited a few more seconds, then slammed my fists into the door.

Faster shuffling. "What the fuck do you want?"

The door opened a crack so he could look out.

I threw myself against the door. It connected with the side of his head, and the gun he held flew out of his hands. As I bum-rushed inside, I grabbed the gun from the floor and tackled him to the ground. Gun to his head, I asked, "Anyone else here?"

He shook his head.

"You sure?"

He nodded.

I kept the gun trained on him and walked him into the kitchen. Told him to sit down in one of the chairs. Using a kitchen towel I found on the oven handle, I tied him to the chair. There was a radio in the kitchen. I turned it on, loud.

I slipped his gun into my coat pocket, and took out my own: .44 Llama. I preferred my own gun to someone else's. I wasn't going to use it right away. I needed answers, and I didn't want him bleeding all over the place. I wanted him focused.

I grabbed a butcher knife from the countertop and placed it on one of the stove burners. Turned the burner on. The knife warmed up.

"Someone tried to slump me today," I said. "You have any idea who might have wanted to do that to me?"

"No." He didn't sound confident. Maybe he knew something, maybe he didn't.

There was no motivation yet. He had no reason to give me a straight answer. I was prepared for this eventuality though. I had a plan.

I slid on an oven mitt and grabbed the knife handle. The blade had a dull orange glow. I approached him. Rested my knee on his legs to gain a little leverage as I leaned my frame toward him. I pressed the knife to his right cheek. "Are you sure you don't know anything about it?"

Grimacing in pain, he said, "No."

He was slightly less confident that time.

I pulled the knife off his cheek and brought it back to the stove. It heated up again. I stared at him and he stared right back at me. I had to give him credit: he had a set of balls.

I took the knife, orange-hot once again, and walked back over to him. I pressed the knife to his ear.

"Are you sure?" I repeated.

The tune changed.

"I don't know," he whimpered. "I don't know."

I pressed the knife harder against his ear. Waiting.

"All I heard is some motherfucker got a call from someone saying you're in possession of some money and coke."

I walked back toward the stove. "Who made that call?"

"I don't know."

I nodded as I heated the knife again.

He looked ready to wet himself from fear. He was not as ballsy as he seemed. I don't believe in violence for the sake of violence. If I could get the answers to my questions without this hot knife, I'd do it. So I tried.

"Who was it that made the call? Who is sharing my business?"

He shook his head. "I don't know anything else."

He was lying.

Or maybe not, but he certainly wasn't telling me everything. There was little time to try to ask the right questions. I picked up the knife.

"Who?" I pressed the edge of the blade against his left eye, letting it cook his eyelid. "Who the fuck made the call?"

He was crying. "I really don't know. Some female. Said she saw the coke. Assumed the money was there. I don't know who."

He screamed as I pressed the knife a little harder.

Then I stood up, threw the knife into the sink, and pulled out my gun.

I looked at him, all fucked up, burnt in several places, but I couldn't feel bad for him. He still knew so much more than he was telling me, but I wasn't going to get anything else from him.

I put the radio on max volume and shot him eight times.

His hands.

Feet.

Ankles.

Wrists.

Shooting someone in the kneecap won't get you answers, but it certainly will send a good message.

I kept my eye on him as I made my way to the door, pulling it closed, then I ran down the stairs and out of the building and to my car. I couldn't be completely sure, but something he said planted the seed of an idea in my head. An idea that I was definitely not happy about considering.

11

TASHA

I'D KNOWN her for a little while. It wasn't forever, and it wasn't a significantly long time. But it wasn't nothing.

I grew to trust her. It made sense. She was often around when my crew and I were taking care of business--at least in the sense that she was keeping watch. She made herself trustworthy. I had no reason, whatsoever, to think otherwise.

This is why I put her up in the apartment. This is why I was paying for groceries. This is why I was taking care of her.

Which is why, when I'd heard that it was a female that sold me out about the robbery, I was upset.

I didn't have a shred of proof while I drove back to the apartment. All I had was some guy's word. Of course, that word came after having a very hot knife put in his eye, but still, I wasn't convinced.

I didn't want it to be true. I wanted her to be someone I could continue to rely on, someone I knew had my back. I was growing very fond of her. I'd dropped Inez, in part, because of Tasha. Because of the feelings I had about her. I wanted to keep Inez safe--that was completely true--but I am a one-woman

man. I knew where things were headed with Tasha and didn't want to hurt Inez. I wanted to protect her from everything, not just bullets, though I didn't do a very good job of that. But it might have been Tasha's fault.

I tried to protect one only to have the other throw a wrench into the works.

Needless to say, I was discombobulated. I had no idea what to think. Everything told me that it was likely Tasha who gave up information to the shooters. At the same time, everything felt like it shouldn't be her.

I don't easily put my trust in people, so when I decided I was going to trust Tasha, I meant it. But she had potentially betrayed me. For most people, there is no forgiveness. Betrayal is the chief sin one can not commit against me. Fire bullets, try to stab me, or throw a punch, I can deal with those things. But lie to me? Betray my trust? That's worse than anything else, which is what made the situation with Tasha so different.

I knew certain things about Tasha. For instance, I knew that Scully was her cousin. He was the one who initially set her up with the old crew, introducing us and having her work as our lookout. I also knew that Scully likely thought I'd fucked him when I left the old crew behind.

Looking back, the connections were there, but my mind didn't want to see them when I was driving home.

WALKING BACK and forth down the aisles of the grocery store, Tasha kept consulting the list Jimmy had given her. She didn't want to make any mistakes. She really cared about Jimmy, and wanted to keep him happy.

Tasha took her time looking over the products before

placing them in the cart. Still, she wanted to get back to the apartment. She felt safe there. Secure.

Jimmy was protecting Tasha safe after taking an interest in her. She liked this. Because of his kindness, she didn't want to disappoint him. Tasha believed part of her job in looking after the apartment was to look after Jimmy when he was there. She took this part seriously.

Tasha was conflicted in her thoughts about him. She knew that he was completely serious about his business and pulled no punches when it came to making money. But being as close as they had been lately--Tasha shuddered as she recalled the pleasure--was different.

This new dilemma she found herself in ate away at her, which only made things worse.

Tasha could see herself with him. Of all the guys she'd seen coming into and out of that old building, he was the only one she ever fantasized about. But she also recognized the danger that came with his lifestyle. Just by being with him, she could get in trouble. A bullet wouldn't discriminate between Jimmy or his woman, and if someone really wanted to get to Jimmy, they could always try to do it through her.

That problem she understood completely.

Tasha had gotten herself close to Jimmy. It was easier than she thought it might be. Much as she may have fantasized about him, she never, ever, not in a million years, expected that he had any interest in her. But apparently he did.

He ended his relationship, to be with me, Tasha thought. *I'm not just some side piece. It wasn't just about sex.*

Tasha wouldn't feel so conflicted if the relationship was just physical. But Jimmy cared about her. And as she added the last item on the list to the shopping cart, walking towards check-out, she knew that she cared about him too.

Standing in line at the checkout, Tasha didn't care what

anyone else in the world needed, she just wanted to be there for Jimmy.

But that couldn't be everything. It was more complicated than that. There were outside influences that affected everything that Tasha did. These influences were big.

Huge.

Massive.

To start, her cousin Scully had a tight hold over her, and he wasn't going to let go anytime soon.

Unless...

She didn't want to think about it.

It wasn't complicated. It was one of the simplest things in the world to do. It was something she did almost all the time. But in this circumstance, it was so incredibly difficult.

Groceries paid for, Tasha walked out to the car. She was ready to return to the apartment and fix a nice dinner for two. That's when Tasha realized she cared more for Jimmy than she ever would Scully. Even if they were not romantically or physically intertwined, even if they were just friends, she would still care more for Jimmy than her cousin.

The reason was clear: Jimmy would never do what Scully had been doing.

A few years back, Tasha had a child. Because of the circumstances she found herself in, Scully's mother took legal custody of the child. Tasha was in a better position now, even without Jimmy's help, but Scully's mother would not relinquish custody.

Tasha begged Scully and his mother.

Neither relented, but Scully would dangle the custody in front of Tasha, like a carrot before a horse, to get her to do something he wanted done.

Only this time was different.

Scully told Tasha she could get custody back. There was

nothing new there. Except this time, Scully's mother agreed too.

The first step of the plan, Scully told her, *is to get close to Jimmy.*

Tasha hadn't done this out of any loyalty to her cousin. She hadn't even attempted it on her own. Jimmy was the one who approached her. Jimmy was the one who took her to the apartment. Jimmy let her live there. But, regardless of how it happened, Tasha had gotten close to Jimmy.

At the beginning, it was too early to tell Scully this. He would never believe that it happened so quickly. He would think Tasha was lying just to get custody back.

So, she waited.

Waited long enough to make sure Scully believed.

And when it came to step two, the only other step, it was so simple, yet so incredibly difficult.

All she had to do was make a phone call. Relay a few small pieces of information. And wait.

It was agonizing.

Tasha struggled for hours trying to decide whether or not to do it. In the end, she believed that whatever this was going to be, Jimmy would understand. He would see her dilemma and understand why she made the choice she did. She knew the softer, caring, kind side of Jimmy.

Tasha was still scared shitless of the other side. The side that the rumors and legends were created by. She was deathly afraid of someone who could stick their fingers in a shotgun to ward off getting killed. She was horrified by someone who could be as ruthless and cold as Jimmy was said to be.

But her kid was her kid, and Tasha wanted him back.

She knew that Scully didn't have Jimmy's best interests at heart. She knew Scully blamed Jimmy for his brother's death. She knew there had been bad blood between the two of them.

But she also knew that they had worked together a few times. They both had done a few licks and shared in the spoils afterwards. Tasha figured that meant something. She figured that her cousin, as much as he had acted like a piece of shit regarding custody, was only trying to show Jimmy up.

A short while after the shooting though, Tasha had heard the details, realized what she had done, and she called her cousin, furious. "What the fuck, Scully? I don't wanna be a part of some shit like that!"

I WALKED from my car to the building. From the entrance to the apartment door. Took out my key.

All I wanted was to be wrong about Tasha. I wanted her to be uninvolved. I was prepared, however, to confront her. As soon as I walked in, that was going to be the first order of business.

I unlocked the door and stepped into the apartment. Tasha was not out front, but she was loud enough to be heard from the bedroom. "I did what you asked me to do."

I paused.

"I made the call. But what the fuck? You tried to have him killed! I didn't know that was part of the plan!"

I was dumbfounded as I stood in the doorway. *Part of the plan*, she said. A plan. She was in on the plan.

I was fuming.

I was livid.

I was a millisecond away from storming into the bedroom and letting every single bit of aggression out on her.

But what she said next stopped me in my tracks.

"I want custody of him now."

Custody of who? I wondered.

"You motherfucker!" She screamed. "You swore to me. Swore to me that I make this call, you'll get your mother to give custody back to me. This has gone on for too fucking long."

There was a pause.

When Tasha spoke again, her anger dissipated and was replaced by sobs. "I can't. I just can't. You made a promise. You told me I could have my son back. I'm not gonna help with anything else. It's done." She sniffled. "You're clearly never going to do what you keep promising. I don't need to do anything else. Never again."

Tasha slammed the phone down as I pushed open the bedroom door.

She wasn't looking in my direction. I could have screamed, yelled, ran at her. But I didn't.

My initial fear was right. But it was also wrong. Someone else was actually responsible. What I heard on the phone didn't absolve Tasha of her role in the shooting earlier today, but I needed more information before making a decision.

I cleared my throat.

She turned. Saw me. For a moment, abject fear washed over her eyes. But then, she jumped up and ran to me.

"Oh my God!" She shouted. "Oh my God! You're okay! Are you okay? I'm so sorry. You're really okay? Oh my God! I'm so sorry. I'm so so sorry. Please forgive me. Please! But you're okay?"

The words fell out of her, blubbering as she tried to touch and hug me. I didn't let her, but I didn't turn away from her either.

When Tasha finally calmed down, she looked up at me. There was still fear in her eyes, but it wasn't that same miserable fear of physical pain or violence that I had initially seen. It was the fear that she had irrevocably destroyed our relationship, mixed in with an intense sadness. A pitiful look.

It broke me.

Her whole reaction to my appearance in the room. Running to see if I was okay. Her complete devastation at what she had done. Her words on the phone. All of it had taken its toll.

"I'm okay," I finally said. "But you need to explain quite a bit before I'm completely okay."

12

TAKEOVER

AFTER DEALING with all the bullshit that came up from the lick--getting shot at, taking care of Inez, confronting Tasha--after all of that, it was finally time to put the product out on the streets.

I don't like drugs. Not a bit. They lead to all sorts of problems I didn't want to deal with. But at this point, I had little choice in the matter. The proverbial cat was out of the bag; it was known that my hands were on this merch. To the general public, it didn't matter if it was stolen or if I'd gotten it through the correct channels. Word on the street was that I had the stuff. That meant I needed to get rid of it.

It was time to get the ball rolling on my larger venture. I might have had these bricks, but nothing was making me money. I had no real income to speak of. Everything was costing me something.

This was a necessary evil though. Starting a new business venture required cracking a few eggs, but how much I needed to crack was throwing me for a loop. I was not yet seeing any returns. It felt like I was eating like an elephant while shitting like an ant.

What I'd gotten from the lick was a good start, but it was hardly sufficient for what I was trying to do. Two bricks would make me a little bit of money, but not top dog. Neither were the additional two bricks that I got on consignment from Bull. But put together the four keys gave me some room to move around the streets and spread my business a little more.

I wasn't happy beginning the venture with powder on consignment, and I wasn't fond about peddling drugs either, but this was the start of something larger. I had the money to buy both bricks from Bull, but he insisted that I take them on consignment as we started our business venture. I could see why.

Bull wanted to see what I'd do, how quickly I could move the product, and how forthright I'd be with his cash. He was figuring me out as a business partner as I was him. Bull knew I wasn't happy about doing it--I can't imagine for a minute that he would be if the roles were reversed--but I did it anyway.

It was important to start off on the right foot. You have to give a little to get a little. If this is how Bull wanted to establish our business relationship, so be it.

As it was time to make some moves, I called Demus up to meet so we could start putting the plan in place. We figured out all the logistics. Now was the time to start the implementation phase.

He showed up later that day in a Ford Taurus. We primarily used it as a transport vehicle. It had this exquisite built-in stash spot that very few people knew about. With no effort on the owner's part, you had a spot sufficient to stash a brick and a half, nearly forty thousand in cash, and two guns I kept in there at all times.

It also helped that the car didn't stand out. Nearly everywhere you looked on the road was a Taurus. Mine might not have completely blended in with the drab colors of all the rest, but it was the same car that seemingly half the US population was driving.

Merely by getting in this car, I was doing something I usually never did. I made it my business never to get into a vehicle that I knew had drugs hidden within. I avoided this at all costs. The last thing I needed was getting pulled over with concealed drugs in the car. But today, I had no choice but to throw caution to the wind. By putting this plan in place, I had to get my hands dirty. It was a calculated risk, but my hope--and expectation--was that it would provide a massive reward.

As Demus drove, my beeper went off. It was Ozzie. I was mildly concerned about his persistence, but since he wasn't necessary for today's part of the plan, he could wait. None of his pages were coming across "911," so I knew it wasn't an emergency. Besides, I saw the sign for East Orange as we drove on 280 and Oranton Parkway, and knew that I couldn't do anything for Ozzie at the moment anyway.

I needed to get mentally prepared for step one of this plan.

We headed to Center Street, a little side street directly behind North Day Street. It was a paradise for this kind of work. You could easily see up and down the entire length of the road, which made looking out for cops or unwanted attention easy.

The street was quiet, and unassuming. The people that lived there kept their mouths shut. It was almost like this little street in New Jersey was made for slinging dope.

I made arrangements to have a quick face-to-face with the main player on the street to discuss his situation. Part of the plan was making sure that the little players stayed in place no matter what. In order for that to happen, I needed to let them know that I was looking out for their best interests.

Never let anyone tell you differently: running anything is the same. Whether it's politics or drugs, if you want to be in charge, the boss, head honcho, el jefe, you need to sell yourself first. What I was doing on Center Street that day was no different than what Jimmy Carter, Ronald Reagan, or George Bush had done to get their job. You're selling the little people--the ones who work for you and support you--a line of bullshit about how much you care about them. In reality, all that matters is your own bottom line.

The guy I was meeting today was a street dealer named Troy.

Today, I'd be his best friend. The next day, I probably wouldn't remember who he was. Just like any politician, any CEO.

We pulled onto Center and saw what passes for action down there: a few dudes sitting around, some playing dice, and not much else.

East Orange was no major city. There were no big players walking its streets. At first glance, you might take this street to be somewhere in suburbia. It was lined with houses, not apartment buildings. It was the projects, but at a quick glance from the outside, you'd never be able to tell.

House music blasted as we drove down the block. Looking around, I started to reminisce a bit. In my earlier years, living in New Jersey, I'd hit a few well-to-do houses on streets that looked just like this one. I'd taken some people for a pretty penny. Part of me longed for that life again. It seemed so much simpler than what I was doing now.

"That's him up there," Demus said as he pulled over and parked the car, shaking me out of pleasant memories.

If things worked out though, the income I had back then wouldn't even compare to what I'd soon make.

I looked up and saw Troy, already aware of his situation.

Troy's supplier was dictating to him what the prices would be and how much he'd sell. This was cutting into Troy's profits. I also knew about the current situation in New Jersey: you either sold coke or you sold heroin. If a customer wanted crack, he'd need to cook it down himself. There was no ready-rock on these streets. Troy needed to deal with all of this. But I could immediately see why his supplier dictated everything.

Troy cared more about his outward appearance than he did about selling product. There's nothing wrong with that, but the fact that Troy wanted to be the center of attention, in every possible way, told me a lot about what I needed to know. He wasn't the kind of person I'd want working for me, but if he was a steady earner that could be taught, perhaps there was a place for him. Troy's *big me, little you* mentality could be a huge detriment, as could his lack of discretion. He barely registered on the totem pole of this life, but perhaps with a little work, he could become someone important. I hoped that was the case since I was bringing him an offer, but I knew that only time would tell. This was a bad first impression though.

Demus walked over to him.

Troy didn't even realize until Demus was standing right in front of him. He was self-absorbed. It was a problem that he didn't register someone approaching. Troy, and all of the people he was absorbed in entertaining, finally looked up at Demus, recognizing someone unfamiliar within their ranks.

Demus leaned over and said something to Troy.

Troy looked over at the car, stood up, adjusted his clothes, and walked over.

Demus motioned for him to get into the front passenger's seat.

He did, and turned to the back where I was sitting. "Jimmy, is that really you?"

"There's no need for that," I said. "This isn't going to take long, and what I'm discussing here is non-negotiable."

"Is that a threat?" He asked nervously.

"No. It's a promise."

"Well," Troy said, sounding a bit more confident, "I know who you are, but I'm no chump, you feel me?"

"Well, my man," I replied, "there's only one letter separating champ from chump, and that's you. But I'm not here to trade insults. I'm here to open doors. If you're interested, that is."

"I'm doing well for myself." Troy puffed himself up, maybe to show off. Maybe to convince himself.

"Is that so?"

He hesitated, thinking, probably afraid to tell the truth. Whatever the reason for his silence, it didn't matter.

This was my meeting.

My discussion.

I didn't need to hear from him. I just needed him to listen to what I was offering and not be a complete idiot. I might have been hoping for too much, considering how Troy carried himself, but I like to believe that if you dangle money in front of someone's face, they're going to be smart enough to take it.

"Here's my offer to you and your crew: your supplier is going to be dismantled. It's either going to happen because he and I reach an understanding, or because he succumbs to the force that I will exert if necessary. Either way, the precedent is going to be set. What I need you to do, is let him know that you are severing all ties with him. You will no longer purchase his product, not for any price. You will not get his product onto the street, between Main Street and Colgate Park, including North Day and Park Avenue."

He nodded, and that alone told me that there was a little more to Troy than I first believed.

"You're going to direct your most loyal customers to my people. In return, I'm going to give you the best price in the area and starve out your competition, so you're going to be able to move more product and quicker."

Troy looked eager.

"Think on this," I continued, "or risk being assimilated. Sever ties with them and get your weight from us."

"Who is 'us?'"

I liked the question. Troy was actually more on the ball than I'd expected. "That's neither here nor there. The point is, there's going to be consistency. Consistency is good for someone like you. It keeps you dressed. It keeps you eating. It keeps you healthy. A lack of consistency is bad for business, you follow?"

After the meeting, and a quick discussion about what we both thought about Troy, Demus and I parted ways.

I stopped at the first payphone I could find and dropped in some coins, waited as the phone on the other end connected, ringing once, twice...

"I need to see you now," Ozzie said.

"When?"

"Right now, if you can."

"Can it wait?"

"No," Ozzie said, in a rush. "All I can say is that time is of the essence."

"I'll be right there."

Damn, I thought while hanging up, *Ozzie sounds annoyed.*

I couldn't imagine what he could be frustrated about. I knew that he wasn't about action. The shootout was evidence of that. He might have been there, but it would have been just as good to have a thirty-pound bag of shit for all he actually did. But he had other attributes, really good qualities. I'd need to find a better role for him. I couldn't count on him in a physical situation--I always knew that--but I might be able to use his mind, his business sense. Something.

I finally pulled up in a pretty posh neighborhood just into Long Island from Queens. It was nicer than I expected. Seemed like Ozzie definitely made that money if he could afford to hole up in a place like this. Bad on the trigger, but good with the bands.

I tried to make it a rule to never underestimate someone, but it seemed like I did that with my new business partner.

The drive here took a lot out of me. I just wanted to go somewhere and crash for a little bit. I'd barely slept, if at all, in the last two days, and now I had to figure out what Ozzie was so keyed up about.

It couldn't be a true emergency. That would have put him much more on edge. The tone of that phone call would have been very different. But this wasn't some picayune thing either.

I knocked on the door expecting Ozzie, but a small built woman answered. She was pretty--really pretty--and wore a friendly smile. I wasn't smitten, but some solid rest and relaxation with her would likely have done me good.

"So, you are him," she said.

"I'm who?" I answered.

"You know, the man who works alone and is hard to find. I've been trying to meet you for a while now."

I laughed. "Seems like I'm at a disadvantage, since you know who I am, but I know nothing about you."

"I'm Ozzie's big sister, Donna."

I smiled, looking her up and down. Nothing about her was big, but she was fine as hell, and everything balanced out really nicely.

"Let in di mon nuh mon," Ozzie yelled from inside.

His sister, Donna, stepped to the side seductively, but

stayed close enough that I had no choice but to brush up against her as I went by.

Once inside, I embraced Ozzie. "What's going on, man?"

"Don't mind Donna," he said.

I took a quick glance over my shoulder, but she was gone.

"She have a thing for you even though she don't know you," Ozzie continued. "She seen you on the streets a time or two, but she's harmless."

Shit, Ozzie, you're harmless too, I thought, chuckling at his explanation. *I'll bet she's got far more bite than you do.*

As he walked me through the house to the den, I noticed that it was pretty lavish. The inside looked exactly as you'd expect from the outside. This wasn't just some hood hidey-hole. This was a home. Something someone would be really proud of. Something you'd pass down to your kids in a Last Will and Testament kind of house. I was impressed.

"Ozzie, I'm tired," I said as we reached the den and sat down. "Let's just get down to brass tacks. What's going on?"

"Alright. You know that area I was tellin' you about? That place where I said we could just slip the product in and be as good as gold, right?"

I nodded.

"I'm not getting the reception I thought I would. As a matter of fact, they just outright denied me entrance. I used your approach, but it didn't fly."

Shit, Ozzie, no bite to you.

This was barely the minor emergency he was making it out to be.

I didn't let the disappointment of these thoughts show. I smiled and stood up. "I'll look into it. Don't worry. I'll figure it out and get back to you. Just sit tight."

He looked disheartened. "You're not upset are you?"

"Nah, man," I lied. "These things happen. That's why we

need to know how to improvise. Who was it you said wasn't letting you in?"

"I never said anyone in particular."

"Right, right. I forgot. Just real tired, Ozzie."

I smiled at him and turned back toward the front door.

On the way out, his sister was there, waiting for me. She pressed paper into my hand. I clutched it and kept walking right through the door.

Before even taking a look at the paper, I jumped back into my car. I wanted to make sure I was somewhere no eyes would be on me. Caution was important. I had no idea what this note was going to tell me, but I wanted to make sure that if someone were looking in my direction, I'd at least be able to get out.

I unfolded the note and read:

Pull up to the corner at the end of the block. I'll be there in five minutes. It is a matter of importance.

I didn't really have time to entertain Donna, but ı was apparently already caught in her web. All it took was that last line to grab my attention. Clearly, she knew something I did not. I needed to find out what it was.

I waited at the corner. It seemed like every car and pedestrian passing by was looking at me. I didn't like to be on display like this, but it was important for me to find out what Donna knew.

Before I realized what was happening, the front passenger door opened, and Donna slipped inside.

I was impressed. She had probably done this before.

"Drive," she commanded.

I looked at her for a moment.

She stared back at me.

I'm no fool, so I did the right thing: I drove.

Donna didn't say much, only giving me directions every once in a while. She seemed to have a destination in mind.

Having lived in New York forever, spending a lot of time in Brooklyn and Queens, I knew where we were going. She had me get on the Belt Parkway headed west.

"Where do you want me to get off?" I asked.

Donna nodded toward the overhead sign. "Take Conduit."

I looked at her a little confused, briefly letting my exhaustion make me believe she wanted me to head to JFK Airport. Now was not the time for a vacation...but, she was a fine looking woman. I took the exit for Conduit Avenue, and just after getting off the highway she indicated for me to go into the JFK Hotel parking lot. I pulled in and found a space.

Donna reached over and opened her door. "I'm going to get us a room. I'll get you when I'm done."

While Donna was gone--no more than five minutes--I kept thinking that this little, petite woman was a force to be reckoned with. She had me wrapped around her finger, driving to wherever, and I never once considered asking her where we were going.

Donna came back to the car, key in hand, and I just shook my head. I let my guard down quickly with this one. But there was a reason. She had information I needed to know. I got out of the car and followed her to the room.

As soon as we got inside, I pulled the .357 Python out of my waist and fell back on the bed.

"Come here," I said.

Donna slid in right beside me and immediately started rubbing my chest. My body awakened to the sensation of her touch. She slowly worked her hands down from my chest to my pants and began stroking my dick through the jeans.

This got me wide awake and standing at attention, which only made Donna happy. There was little pretense as she unzipped my pants, sensuously pulled them and my briefs down, and smiled at what she saw. Pushing her panties aside, she straddled me.

It was just what the doctor ordered.

Donna rode me for all she was worth, setting the pace and refusing to let me do anything except lay there and be fucked. Every time I tried, she pushed me back down. She rode up and down and up and down, loving every second of it. After some time, she stopped, and started massaging me with the muscles in her pussy. I was in heaven.

Donna slowly started pumping up and down again. She shuddered and spasmed as a massive orgasm hit her. A few seconds later, I exploded inside her.

I WOKE UP, startled by a sound, and automatically reached for my gun. I felt the cold blue steel and relaxed a little bit, but before I could really breathe easily, I opened the chamber and saw six bullets in there. Lethality in my hand. When I looked up from the gun, I saw Donna staring at me with a wicked smile on her face as she looked at my dick, stuck to my thigh.

I slowly got out of the bed and walked over to the window, glancing outside to notice it had grown dark. "What time is it?"

She looked over at the bedside clock. "11:15."

Damn, I thought, *I slept the whole day away.*

I should be out doing my nocturnal prowling, not laid in a hotel bed. I hated getting side-tracked.

"What's this matter of importance?" I asked.

"My brother isn't going to be able to get you what you want. But I can."

"And how exactly are you going to do that?"

She smirked. "I used to date the main guy around there, and every now and then, I throw him a pity fuck. He thinks it's more than that, so he trusts me. But he's also violent. Can't keep his hands to himself."

"Look Donna, I've got two questions. First, you make like you know all this shit about me, so what exactly is it that you know, or have heard? Second, what are you getting out of all this?"

She patted her belly. "What I'm getting out of all this is swimming inside me right now."

Shit. Damn girl took advantage of my exhausted state.

Got the whole ravioli with some extra sauce.

"I've heard that you're a vicious killer. You took some big scores. I heard you're both the muscle and the brain. You go from one extreme to the next."

"Don't believe everything you hear," I responded.

"You don't move in a way that contradicts anything I heard," she shot back. "I've done nothing but watch you, all day. You're what they say you are. It's not normal for someone to wake up the way you just did."

I smiled. "Alright. Fine. Set this dude up for me. I'll make sure nothing blows back on you."

"I've got no problem with it, but I do have a problem fucking him. I've got no interest in doing that."

"You can do this without that. You said he trusts you. That's a good thing. But right now, I need you to trust me. You trust me, right?"

She nodded.

"I need you to set up a meet with him. Tell me where you're gonna be. Pick a place where there won't be too many people. But understand, when I roll through and do what I need to do, I have to make it look real. You're gonna need to be as much a victim as he is. Can you handle that? Cause I need to know you can and will."

"I will. I promise."

"All right. I'll make sure there's something in it for you when we're done."

———

"THERE THEY ARE," Demus said, pointing down the block.

"Are they alone?" I asked.

"Yeah."

Demus and I stepped out of the black Honda Prelude, heading in the direction of Donna and Smooth--the guy she was helping set up.

Demus and I were both in ski masks. No one was around, but this was no time for making errors in judgment. I scanned the block one more time, then pulled my pistol out. Smooth was a reputable street player quick to buss his own gun. He must have felt Demus on him, because he reached for his waist before spinning around. He wasn't fast enough making his pirouette, and had a Desert Eagle to his temple.

"If you know what's good for you..." Demus didn't need to finish as Smooth handed over his gun.

At the same time, I swung the .357 across Donna's shoulder.

She screamed and hit the ground.

"Bitch, shut the fuck up," I growled.

She grabbed her shoulder, crying in earnest.

Demus and I marched them back into the building they were standing outside of. Demus had the muzzle of his gun pressed into Smooth's side. My gun was aimed at Donna's kidney. We got them into the elevator and up to the fourth floor, straight for Smooth's apartment, who was dumbfounded at how we knew where he holed up.

"Open it," Demus said, shoving him forward with the gun. "Don't make me say it twice."

"Do you know who I am?" Smooth asked.

I was impressed. There was only the tiniest, imperceptible hint of fear in his voice.

"You're making a major mistake," he said. "Walk the fuck away now, before this gets any worse for you."

Demus smiled and cracked Smooth across the head with the butt of the Desert Eagle. Smooth's knees buckled. He nearly went down as some blood started to trickle from his head.

"Let's try this one more time," Demus said to him. "Open. The. Door."

Donna whimpered in my hands.

"Bitch, make one more sound and I'll knock you're fucking teeth in," I said.

Smooth unlocked the door and we all stepped inside.

"Where's the money?" I asked.

"What money?" Smooth relied.

I smacked Donna across the face. Gave her a swift kick to the ribs after she fell to the floor. She curled up in the fetal position.

"Where is the money?" I repeated.

"All I've got is $25,000 in the bedroom closet." There was more fear in his voice. "That's it. I swear."

Demus tied him up to a chair and went to check the bedroom closet. He returned a minute later with the cash, some jewelry, a diamond watch, and a herringbone chain.

"This ain't money," Demus said. "Where's the fuckin' bank roll and whatever else passes for value?"

"I've got nothing else," Smooth whimpered.

I kicked Donna once more in the ribs, then lifted her up and carried her to the bedroom, kicking the door close.

"Beg and plead, girlie," I whispered. "Make it sound real."

She turned to me then screamed, "No, please, no. Don't!"

"Shut up, bitch!" I pulled down her pants and took off her panties. She was soaking wet. I rubbed the panties' crotch against her bloody shoulder. Then I started to fuck her. "Oh, damn, this is some fine pussy."

"No, no! Stop!" She screamed as she turned to smile at me.

After about ten minutes, she convulsed on the floor, coming like crazy as I blew my own load deep inside her. I pulled out, zipped up my pants, leaving Donna on the floor as I walked back out and threw her bloody panties at Smooth.

He was sickened.

"I'm not asking again. Where's the fucking money?"

He trembled. "I've got another fifteen in the bathroom closet along with the rest of my product."

Once Demus got everything, we secured both of them in separate rooms.

Donna, while bloody, was laying on the floor of the bedroom with a shit-eating grin on her face.

"I told you I had to make it believable," I said.

"It was incredible," she whispered.

I smiled. "Keep playing the role. Don't contact me. Everything's gonna work out. But don't mention shit to your brother."

She nodded.

Demus and I left with a duffle bag filled with money and drugs as we hopped back in the Honda. Before stopping back at our place, Demus pulled over to a payphone. I got out and called Ozzie.

"Yo, my man," I said, "try that spot again. Give it a day or two, but I think you got it in you to change their minds."

13

HUSTLER

IT HAD BEEN months since I'd felt the cold steel pressed against my temple on that street in East Orange. I had made a decision that I would never again find myself in that kind of situation. I would do any and everything I could to ensure that I was the one holding the gun, and not be on the receiving end. But this was going to require work.

Having a little kid on the street become someone who had his name echo down that same area, causing people to tremble just at the mere sound of it, wasn't going to happen overnight. I intended, I desired, to be a man that would and could instill fear in the hearts of respectable men. But it was going to take some time.

I spent the last several months building a bit of a name for myself, doing odd jobs here and there for well-known people. I was making good money. I was also vicious. I was hungry to succeed and advance. Because of that, I showed no fear. I did what was needed to make it clear I was a force to be reckoned with.

I was an anomaly. I was young--really young--making big money. I was afraid of nothing. I confused others.

People would see me coming down the street, and their initial thought was, *Who the fuck does this young punk think he is?*

Once they saw me in action, getting a taste of my aggression, they no longer thought of me as some young punk. Despite my growing reputation, there were still those who didn't know I was someone not to be messed with until after the fact.

I spent a lot of my time, however, slinging drugs.

I enjoyed the prestige that came with that kind of lifestyle--money, guns, women--but this wasn't a long-term goal for me. I didn't want to get caught up in the world of selling dope. It was too easy to get caught, too easy to lose money, and too easy to end up on the wrong side of a gun.

I started, like most dealers, by selling weed here and there. Eventually, I graduated to powder cocaine and dabbled in selling heroin. I saw huge returns. Despite the money, I was unhappy with what I was doing.

I didn't like dealing with so many different people, nor did I like the idea that there were hundreds of people who knew me on sight. I wanted to blend into the shadows. I wanted anonymity and obscurity. I wanted to be the guy that was always talked about, but never seen. I wanted to be Keyser Soze or the Dread Pirate Roberts. I wanted the name without the face.

Plus, I had another hustle that was keeping me from the 24-hour world of selling drugs. This other occupation was more my speed and far more interesting to me. It required intelligence, planning, precision, fearlessness, and the ability to think on your feet.

Call it what you will: robberies, licks, juks, spot rushing, heists, scores. It might sound simple, but without the smarts to think and plan, it was not something you could be successful at. I lived for rushing in, grabbing loot, and heading out. I was as good as a Viking, plundering and pillaging. I didn't need to be distracted by standing out on a corner passing dime bags. I needed to stay sharp and continue to hone my craft.

I was often going after guys way bigger than me--guys who were known and respected all over--and needed to keep a level head on the street to make sure my other occupation wasn't known. I needed to be in the shadows. Last thing I wanted was people to see me living beyond my means. I made a good scratch selling, but I would make much much more from just one lick.

There was also the thrill I would get from holding these bigger dudes at gunpoint, making them completely powerless. Any other time, these guys wouldn't hesitate to kill, abduct, or maim to get their point across. But when I rushed in on them and had my gun out, they were lambs.

The adrenaline rush from that alone was my drug.

There was a level of fear too. I'd be an idiot to say that I was never afraid whatsoever. I was running into places manned by reputable crews who were all armed and dangerous in their own right. But I put that fear aside, knowing that I was smarter, stealthier, and simply better than they were.

I did my homework before doing any of these jobs, spending my days plotting, planning, securing, and strategizing, considering every circumstance.

I knew the best time to hit a spot. I knew when there would be the fewest guys there. I knew when they would have the most available for the taking. Some crews were smart enough to only have large amounts of cash, drugs, jewels, on hand when there was an equally large group of people to protect it. Others weren't.

The downside is that the slightest miscalculation could cost a life, whether it be yourself or the lives of people you care about.

Inevitably, you want to protect the people robbing places with you. You're in it together. If one of you gets hurt, it's probably going to be bad for you as well. There is no safety net. A moment's hesitation or indecision can cost you dearly.

It was always important for me to plan, plan, and plan. When I was done planning, I would plan a little bit more. I was meticulous.

I started robbing people and places young.

At first it was small stuff: Cuban links, herringbone necklaces, Rolexes, diamond rings, rope chains. Eventually I was kicking in doors, holding people at gunpoint, and relieving them of their merchandise. It wasn't until I got older when I started specifically targeting drug dealers. The risk was high, but it was well worth it for the potential rewards.

At sixteen, I was already driving, but the car that I had--a sky blue Toyota Cressida--typically stood out like a sore thumb. Not only was the color unique, but it had deeply tinted windows and a booming sound system. Much as I loved the car, I didn't like driving it around too often. It violated my belief of being inconspicuous.

To prevent it from interfering with my chosen occupation, I would use innocuous cars I had access to. They weren't mine, so to speak, as they belonged to people I was close with, who wouldn't mind if I borrowed one. Most of the cars I used were pretty nondescript, like the blue Honda Prelude.It didn't stand out in a crowd and was perfect for moving around in the shadows

On occasions, I would hang out in Colgate Park in Orange, New Jersey, during the wintertime of the year. I enjoyed the cold weather, prefering to be outside when it was just around freezing rather than the hot days of summer. Colgate Park was known as a drug hub. If you wanted something, it was almost guaranteed that you could find it there. I held two different shifts in the park where only my product was sold.

I always made sure I had a lot of powder cocaine and at least a full day's supply of weed. I had a small group of under-lings--younger kids--who were moving some of the product for me. On top of that, I had two good-looking females pushing the weed for me. For my part, I just hung out on the bleachers watching my business interests, keeping a concealable 25 caliber on me at all times. This nice and dangerous bit of insurance was there mostly to be just that: insurance. I didn't so much need it to protect myself, but I wanted the people pushing for me to feel protected.

One day, while sitting on the bleachers, I reached an epiphany about the drug trade. It was exceptionally lucrative, that much was obvious, but there were too many ups and downs. Too many risks.

I could deal with the risks though, I just didn't like the fact that selling drugs by itself wasn't going to get you anywhere. This was not the path to success or financial security.

On the news, we see stories of people like Pablo Escobar or El Chapo, and think that all drug dealers are banking tons of cash. But that's not the case. Yeah, the guys running the cartels live in houses built with bricks of cash, but if any street-level dealer--or even a guy supplying a large area--tells you that he's getting rich just off selling drugs, he's a motherfucking liar.

If you believe you're gonna flip an ounce of coke into a life of selling keys, I've got a bridge to sell you...and probably a padded room to throw you in with the other lunatics.

That's not to say it can't be done, but it requires a huge amount of luck. Not skill. Not talent. Not smarts. But luck. Between controlled buys, wiretaps, surveillance, robberies, snitches, competition, violence, and a wealth of other factors, you need to be one lucky son of a bitch to make that happen, and being that lucky requires luck on its own. Simply put, it's not happening.

I came to that realization sitting on the bleachers in Colgate Park, and decided to give up the drug game. The juks that I was already doing were bringing in real money, and were bringing it in fast. If I focused more of my time and effort on that, I'd definitely be making bank. Whatever I might have made from selling coke and weed in a day, I could easily triple that just from one job.

So, I invested in my trade.

I spent a bit of time doing practice runs on smaller-time guys. I learned from every job I did. If I planned for x but y happened, I would account for both next time. If I learned that Tuesday was the best day to hit a particular spot, I'd make it so I'd be there on Tuesday. If the job called for three people to handle the situation, l made sure to select my best three. If it needed four, I'd find an equally good fourth.

Whether the take was massive or just a handful, I knew that I was getting something, and it gave me the adrenaline rush I wanted. I tried to stay away from taking jewelry or flashy items from people. These items showed a person's status in the drug totem pole, and it meant something to them, as it took a lot of hustling to acquire. Plus, since I was trying to do all of this under the radar to make sure no one knew Jimmy robbed them, I wasn't about to wear any of that stuff.

Instead, I did my homework to learn who the biggest players were by focusing on areas that had massive amounts of weight, or large stores of cash. I hit those places, as peacefully as I could, and relieved them of those valuables. Drugs were easy to get rid of, and cash was cash. It took time, but over the years, I put together a crew where everyone had the individual skills needed to best get the job done. There was some trial and error finding these kinds of guys.

But sometimes, the universe just sends you a sign.

I HAD this one dealer in my sights for a long time. He wasn't top dog, but he was big time. I knew that I would be able to get out with a big score if I hit him right. From what I'd come to understand, tonight would be the best time to hit him for the optimal payout.

Of course, other people were doing the same homework.

I drove the Prelude and parked it on Halstead Street, a block over from North Taylor. I walked back to the building. The guy I was looking for drove a blue Mitsubishi Gallant with a black rag top. When I saw it parked on the street out front of the building, I knew he would be there with the massive stash.

I headed inside. The elevator was already on its way up, so I took the stairs two at a time to get to the seventh floor. I paused for a minute to catch my breath, then stepped out into the hallway, making my way to the apartment.

I knew there would be no more than three people inside. Even though I was alone, I was ready. I knew who would be there, where they all would be, and how best to subdue them.

I had my gun out, inching down the hallway toward the apartment door.

I needed to be quiet. I didn't want to spook anyone, especially not the people in 7C. I needed 7C and all of its occupants to have no idea I was here. I did all of my homework. I prepared for every eventuality...except one. Another dude, dressed all in black, creeping toward the same apartment.

We noticed each other at the same moment.

He had a gun. I had a gun.

Both of us aimed at each other.

I took a step closer. He took a step closer. Neither of us dared fire the guns, because all that would do is arouse the people in 7C. Neither of us wanted that. But we kept inching to each other. It was like watching Lucille Ball do the mirror routine with Harpo Marx.

I stepped. He stepped.

I looked around. He looked around.

I repositioned the gun. He repositioned the gun.

Finally, close enough to speak in hushed tones, he whispered, "What the fuck are you doing?"

"Same thing you are."

He shook his head. "This is my lick. You're outta luck."

"The fuck I am. I've been doing my homework on this guy for weeks."

He rolled his eyes and shrugged; he had done the same.

After a very pregnant pause, I broke the ice. "We're at a stalemate."

He nodded.

"Thoughts?" I was stalling for a little bit of time. I wanted to think this through. How could I get rid of him, quickly and quietly, and continue with this job?

"We go in together," he said.

I was taken aback.

It wasn't a terrible idea. It had briefly entered my mind as well, but I dismissed it as both impossible and implausible. There was certainly enough in the apartment for me to split it with someone, but I didn't want to deal with the hassle. Especially with someone I'd never met before.

Could I trust him?

He motioned me to follow him to another stairway. I wasn't too keen about following someone blindly into a confined space, but when he put his gun down--still carrying it in his hand--and turned his back to me, I figured it was the least I could do. If I was a different kind of person, I might have shot him right there, just for sheer stupidity. But I'm not.

We stepped into the stairwell.

"We both clearly did our homework," he said. "We both clearly know it's a big score. We could fight, raise hell out here, and both lose out, or--"

"We go in together."

"And split everything 50-50," he added.

I nodded.

"You need to follow my lead."

I chuckled. "That's not how I work. I don't follow. This isn't my first go around. And let's face facts," I nodded at my gun, "I've still got a gun pointed at you."

He shrugged. "Probably not my smartest move." Then he smiled and held out his hand. "Demus."

Still aiming at him, I shook it. "Jimmy."

"Alright, Jimmy, what's the play?"

I lowered the gun.

AFTER WE SPLIT the take from the apartment, we both realized that we were onto something. Teaming up would get us bigger takes and more frequent jobs. The potential was exceptionally lucrative.

A friendship immediately blossomed.

I saw something in him that was valuable, but I also respected that he was able to think on his feet and turn a completely shitty situation into something good. I knew that Demus had a good head on his shoulders. I had a solid role in mind for him, working with me, but I still needed to make sure he could be relied upon.

We grabbed a bite at a local Jamaican spot and talked over beef patties and oxtail with rice and peas. I drank a Ting, he had a Kola Champagne. Eventually, I steered the conversation to our mutual occupation. I asked Demus if he had any solid leads on other guys who were serious about playing Robin Hood, minus giving back to the poor. He explained that he could point me in the right direction, but he wouldn't be an active participant. Seeing my frustration by the turn of events, Demus told me he had much respect for me, and I could count on him in the clutch. He'd have my back, and promised to always be available to take care of other shit for me if need be. I appreciated his honesty.

After exchanging beeper numbers, we shook hands and parted ways, leaving not just as friends, but as silent partners with the understanding that he would always be on call.

14

UNTOUCHABLE

I SPENT most of my time traveling between three different places: Richmond, Virginia; East Orange and Newark, New Jersey; and Brooklyn, New York.

Part of it was for pleasure, most was business. I had a lot of balls in the air, but I was exceptionally good at juggling. It didn't matter what was going on or where, I was on top of everything that was happening. Business was good, money was flowing, and Bull and I found that we worked exceptionally well together.

Life was good. Money was coming in faster than I could even imagine spending it. Most of the time, I was able to just sit back and enjoy things. But only for so long. Eventually, sitting back and enjoying things became problematic. I needed something to do in order to pass time. For me, that meant finding a good lick.

Someone might look at the situation I was in and wonder, *Why on Earth are you still robbing people?*

To answer that question, I pose another: Why not?

I had the means, the skills, and the drive to go do it successfully. I didn't shy away from getting my hands dirty in that regard. So why not?

There were plenty of guys who thought they were better than me, simply by flaunting their valuables. They deserved to get robbed. To be reminded of the fact that no, you are not better than me. You should not flaunt shit in front of my face. You are not untouchable.

A lot of my business dealings were still on the streets though. Particularly in Richmond, where I needed to do quite a bit of juggling to keep things from spinning out of control. I had to deal with wannabe-type-A personalities there, more than anywhere else. A vast majority of my time spent in Richmond was in three different areas: Lynhaven and Drake Street; 31st Street in Church Hill; and the Walmsley Boulevard projects. Each of these spots had their crews--the guys who ran the place before I stepped in and helped them understand who really did.

On the South Side--Lynhaven and Drake--I had to spend some time molding Sluggy and Frog into shape. Sluggy thought of himself as hot shit since he ran the block before I got there, and acted like he was completely untouchable, moving like a guy that had nothing to worry about. The same held true in Church Hill with Stitch, Mikey, and Huggs. Stitch ran that crew while butting heads with people elsewhere, and believed he was king inside the little bubble of his neighborhood. Rodney was the guy on Walmsley Boulevard. He had Burt and Skinner backing him up, but he played the *can't-get-me* game.

All three of these crews, at one time or another, butted heads with each other, and generally didn't get along. This one stepped on that one's turf. This guy sold some dope to that guy's customer. Most of it was petty bullshit. All of it got in the way of business. None of it improved profits or sales. There were too many cooks in these areas, causing the broth to spoil.

Until I showed them who was really meant to be king.

I never entered a situation, especially one as volatile as a hostile takeover, without first doing some homework. I wanted to go after the highest value target first. Not only would it make things easier down the road--at a time when my own forces and resources might be depleted--it was also going to show everyone else what was about to happen.

Having spent plenty of time down in Richmond, I knew a lot of the guys I was about to go against. I even liked some of them. But this was business. And you can't make an omelet without cracking a few eggs. In this kind of business, you can't make good money without cracking a few heads. Didn't matter if I knew the head, or even liked them, it was just about making money.

Sluggy and Frog controlled a majority of the area in Richmond, covering the whole South Side. I needed to go after them first. If I took over a large area, others would worry.

Fortunately, I didn't really know either of these guys much. I'd spoken to them in passing, maybe once or twice. I'd seen them out places. Some of my people knew them.

I wanted to go after Sluggy and Frog with the least amount of collateral damage. I wasn't trying to alert the police of what was happening. Violence was going to be necessary, but I wanted to keep it to a minimum. The last thing I needed was to have cops crawling around everywhere, looking for evidence of some major crimes. Plus, I wanted to keep Sluggy or Frog, preferably both, in place since they already had rapport with the guys under them. Sometimes it's better to maintain the current management than replace it completely.

I could have employed the same strategy I used when helping Ozzie out, but because Sluggy had a larger territory, there needed to be a change in tactics. I had to get Sluggy and Frog alone so they could see that I offered a better deal than their current suppliers, and it was going to require some serious "negotiations." Easier said than done.

Sluggy was not stupid.

Neither was Frog.

They were savvy and hip to things going on around Richmond. They likely would have heard I was in town. I did have a reputation for brazen robberies of high-profile individuals. They fit the category, and were probably on alert for myself and anyone associated with me, so I proceeded like this was a business deal. I decided to reach out for a sit-down.

Of course, Demus volunteered to be the one to relay the message, proving once again that he would walk in front of a bullet for me, which he might have to in order to reach either of these guys. Maybe it should have been me rather than Demus, but he was my number two. It was a show of strength and respect on my end. A direct approach.

We were going to ask them to sit down and discuss a business opportunity. This meeting was going to take place at a mutually agreeable location. It was going to be Demus, myself, and a third of my choosing. The same rules applied for Sluggy and Frog. Three people on both sides. No one else.

We were going to talk like gentlemen. I was coming with an offer, a business opportunity that they could take or leave. Yes, we were all going to be strapped, but the idea was that we didn't need guns. They were smart guys. They would understand a lucrative proposition when they heard one. We would all leave this sit-down as friends, compatriots, comrades, and partners. We were all going to make a ton of money together.

That was what Demus was telling them. I knew better.

Just like they would assume I'd bring two more guys with me, I assumed they would do the same. Of the handful of "mutually agreeable locations" they would choose from, I was going to have people completely unknown in Richmond, in and around these places. I was not walking in blind. While Sluggy might have five or ten guys available, I would make sure I had a few more. This was all a precaution.

If the meeting went as expected, I wouldn't need any of this. If they balked, I'd overwhelm them by sheer numbers and get what I wanted anyway. The context of the meeting was going to be subtle, but it was going to be forceful.

They'd learn it was my way or the highway.

LEAVE it to some wannabe gangsters to be utterly unprepared for when something bad happened. Especially to them. Especially when someone with a name asks them to meet. It was almost like they thought that I was building my empire by buying people out with cash and respect.

They picked the meeting place. They showed up with just three guys in total, though there were two down the street in cars. All of the other spots where they might have felt safe were completely empty. It was me, Demus, and Ozzie. Sluggy and Frog brought a kid who didn't look to be older than thirteen. It was a joke.

I felt sorry for them. Initially, this meeting was going to play out in one of three ways--the only way a meeting like this could possibly go:

1) Walk in guns blazing and take the room.

2) Listen, but ultimately make a lesson out of a couple people in the room.

3) We work it out diplomatically.

I didn't understand why Sluggy came with such little backup. Even if he had the utmost respect for me, even if he believed that I could kill him just by blinking, even if he was the craziest lunatic who ever lived, I still assumed he'd bring more than five guys total.

Could there be more hiding out somewhere else that me and my people aren't aware of? I didn't want there to be trouble, but if there was going to be any, I wanted the upper hand.

I double and triple-checked with Demus before heading inside.

Everything he knew said that it was these five guys. The regulars on the street were on the street. The higher ups--those guys who answered directly to people like Frog or Sluggy--were where they were expected to be. This was either the most perfectly planned set-up ever, or how it was going to play.

With as much confirmation of the facts possible, I decided I was going to change tactics and approach these guys diplomatically, believing it was best to forgo the original plan. Obviously, if they felt comfortable enough to meet, perhaps they were eager to change teams. I had no intent to put down my guard. I recognized the possibility that Sluggy thought that this was a show of force. He might think he looked bigger and badder than me by showing up to this sit-down, essentially, alone.

Unless everything Demus learned was wrong, I had the upper hand.

The meeting spot we walked into seemed cozy enough. A sparsely furnished apartment. Two couches. We sat on the empty one.

"Why'd you wanna meet?" Sluggy asked, as soon as my ass hit the cushion.

No hesitation. I wasn't too keen about that. A small part of me just wanted to cause him some pain. But I held back.

"It's not complicated," I said. "I have the ability to get your supplies cheaper and more easily. I can keep you better supplied, and for less. This means you can make more money. That alone is a win-win situation."

Sluggy looked at Frog, then back to me.

"As those infomercials on TV say," I continued, "'But wait, there's more!'"

"What more?" He was either a complete nincompoop or had no respect whatsoever.

"You get to keep your territory. I don't replace you with my own people. You continue to work, just like you have been. Life goes on, as it always does, but with no changes."

Sluggy was not enthused.

"I really want to sell my drugs on the South Side," I explained. "Really badly. But I want to work with people who are smart enough to see when there is real money to be made. I believed you to be one of those smart people. I really hope that I didn't misjudge you."

"I see," Sluggy said, exchanging a nod and shrug with Frog. "Gimme a minute to talk it over."

I stood up, making a sweeping motion with my hands. "Please, take your time."

Demus and Ozzie followed me into the hallway. I had an idea where this was going when we went back inside.

I nodded to Demus.

He ran down the hallway to the front door of the apartment block. He waved, nodded, then ran back. As he returned, the thirteen-year-old-looking kid opened the door and escorted us back inside. The kid joined Sluggy and Frog on the couch.

We remained standing.

"Sit," Frog said, "no reason to stand."

"All due respect," I said, "but there's no need. You two didn't talk long enough to decide anything. You got no intention of hopping on board anyway, right? Don't feel like making money?"

"Just who in the fuck do you think you are?" Sluggy rose.

He wasn't coming toward Demus, myself, or Ozzie, so I figured I'd let him speak.

"You roll up into my city, come to where I work, and try to tell me that you can do shit better than me? Fuck kinda shit is that?"

I merely nodded as he continued.

"I heard about you. We all heard about you. Big shot motherfucker. So what? Got the nerve to call me an idiot, tell me I'm stupid. You misjudged me. Man who sticks his fingers in a gun ain't none too bright either, ya dig?"

With a quick flick of my eyes towards Demus, he knew what needed to be done. Faster than you could say Jack Robinson, Demus had Sluggy pinned on the floor.

Sluggy struggled, but keeping him down wasn't difficult.

I pulled out my .44 Llama and had it trained on Frog.

The young kid broke left and made a bee-line out the door. Ozzie followed for a few steps, but I called him back. It didn't matter if the young kid was off to get reinforcements. We'd be long gone before anyone else showed up.

"You are a fucking idiot." I spit on Sluggy's face. "Such disrespect for someone crazy enough to stick his fingers in a gun, but no foresight to have a few more of your guys around. You said you heard about me. Fuck made you take me for a pussy then?"

He continued to struggle under Demus. I nodded. Demus pulled out his gun and held the muzzle to his head--right between the eyes.

Sluggy's jeans darkened. When looking at Frog, I saw the same thing. Ozzie, Demus, and I cracked up.

"Some fucking bigshots," Ozzie chuckled.

I nodded at Demus. He pistol whipped Sluggy, drawing a deep gash across his forehead.

I turned to Frog. "Listen up, my man. You see how this

played? You both done pissed yourself. That won't fly." I turned to Sluggy. "Ya dig?"

Sluggy nodded.

"I don't think he digs," I said.

Demus's hand slipped as he pistol whipped Sluggy again, hitting his nose. It was probably broken--I wasn't a doctor--but it certainly was bloody.

"Try to dig this," I said. "I can get you wherever you are. You see that, right? You feel that? You dig?"

At first, Sluggy didn't respond, but when Demus raised the gun again, he nodded furiously. "I dig, man, I dig."

I shrugged, then nodded to Demus, who moved like he was about to get up, but instead slammed his fist into Sluggy's mouth.

A tooth fell out when Sluggy opened his mouth.

"Frog," I said.

He jumped, probably surprised to hear his own name.

"You ever feel like you want to be in charge?" I asked.

Frog glanced at Sluggy, unsure of how to answer.

"Don't worry about him," I said. "He's gonna be out of commission for a while. Someone is going to need to take over. Run things. Make intelligent decisions. You follow me?"

Frog nodded.

"I'm gonna need to hear you say it."

Breathing heavy, snot bubbles popping out his nose as a tear streaked down his cheek, Frog's voice hitched up and down as he spoke. "Are you..." He pointed to Sluggy. "Are you gonna kill him?"

Demus, with a pretty sadistic grin, laughed as he pointed the gun at Sluggy.

"Nah," I chuckled. "Don't plan to. Might not need to. See, all I'm waiting for is someone, really anyone in Sluggy's crew--well, maybe I mean *your* crew--to make just one, single, intelligent decision today. Just one. I figure if we all walk out, you know, win-win, there's nothing to worry about. There'd be no reason to bring further violence to an amicable situation. It would seem counterproductive to the purpose at hand, don't you agree?"

Frog thought about it for a moment, then nodded.

"You could find yourself in a much more advantageous position today," I continued. "But frankly, I am a busy man. I've got a lot of shit to do. I don't really care which one of you agrees, I just need someone to make a decision so that we can move on. To bigger and better things. Now," lowering my gun, I sat down, "it could be you that makes that decision. But be fore-warned, if it is you who does, you'll likely need to deal with the consequences vis a vis your comrade on the floor here."

I casually pointed the gun at a groaning Sluggy.

"I don't know that, even if he agreed to work with me, that I could trust Sluggy over there, just based on previous actions and behaviors. But should you feel ready and willing to enter bold new territories, and handle your own trash, perhaps you and I can come to an agreement?"

WE DID.

Frog was not as stupid as he looked, and knew not to look a gift horse in the mouth. Not only was I offering him what might wind up being a very lucrative deal, but I was also offering him up Sluggy's entire operation and crew on a silver platter. Frog almost agreed even before hearing my terms and conditions.

Having taken care of the South Side, I turned my attention to Church Hill and the Walmsley Projects. Church Hill was bigger--an entire neighborhood--but the projects accounted for a large volume of traffic and sales.

I considered the best ways to deal with offering up my proposition to both Stitch, who oversaw Church Hill, and Rodney, who ran the Walmsley Projects. I am not by nature a violent man. I was known to fly off the handle from time to time when I was younger, but generally, I wanted to handle a situation amicably.

Obviously, the best way was to take the diplomatic approach. Come with respect, friendliness, and a sense of working together. This was easier said than done. It had clearly failed with Sluggy, but he was in a different position since he ran a whole section of the city, unlike Stitch or Rodney.

Rodney and I, however, had a bit of a history. We'd come to fisticuffs a few times in the past, and there was still some bad blood on his part. I was able to look beyond all of that. This was business. That was personal. It had been a few years since I'd seen him, so I hoped he matured as much as I had.

If not, I'd need to be more on my guard than I was with Sluggy. I wasn't happy about that, but we were going to meet and discuss his future, regardless of his feelings toward me.

I decided to save the visit with Rodney for last. Church Hill was bigger and required more moving parts. Logic told me that if I took over Church Hill, Rodney would have very little choice in whether or not to do business with me.

I set the meet with Stitch up the same way I had with Sluggy.

Demus went to present my desire of meeting. They were promised the ability to select the location of the meet, but they were limited in the manpower they'd be allowed. Once again, it would be three of us and three of them.

Demus came back with a bit of surprising news. Stitch was willing to meet the very next day, and he seemed excited. Remembering Sluggy's desire to meet, I immediately went into protection mode.

There were only two reasons Stitch would be excited to meet: first, he'd already heard about what went down with Sluggy, so he wanted to sit down, agree to my terms, and continue working; second, he was preparing an ambush for the meeting. By agreeing to meet, there was a good chance that Demus, Ozzie, and I were walking into a trap. But as the requester of the meet, I was obliged to show once he'd agreed.

We met the following day in a small house in Church Hill. It looked abandoned. The shutters were hanging on by single screws, the paint was peeling, and the floor of the small porch sagged a few inches when you stepped on it. The floorboards inside weren't much better. It felt like walking into a deathtrap.

In the kitchen were Stitch, Mikey, and Huggs, drinking coffee.

I'd seen enough mafia movies to know that when you show up to a meet and the opposite side is casually drinking coffee, it might be wise to check out the rest of the place. With a small nod to Demus, I sent him off to do just that.

Stitch offered Ozzie and I coffee. We both looked at each other confused. A beer, maybe. Some cognac, more likely. Hell, even fruit punch would have been a more natural choice for this kind of meeting. But coffee? We both declined. Stitch didn't seem to mind.

Demus returned--the house was tiny--and reported nothing out of the ordinary. There were no couches. Really, there was no furniture at all. There were kitchen cabinets and a small counter. Each party stood on opposite sides of the counter.

"Jimmy, it's good to see you," Stitch said. "I gotta say, I'm really surprised you wanted to meet."

"Why's that?" My guard was still up. He may have begun the conversation more politely than Sluggy did, but that didn't mean anything in a situation like this.

"This is a pretty small neighborhood. Yeah, we make

decent money. Keep ourselves happy, but a guy who moves like you? Wanting to talk to us? Especially after what you did with Sluggy. I just wasn't expecting it. I figured you'd look right over us here in Church Hill."

I wasn't digging this self-deprecation. It certainly wasn't charming, or business-savvy. It made him look like a rube, but it also made me wonder if he had something up his sleeve. Rather than relaxing me, it created a deeper concern.

"Look Stitch," I said, "you do good business around here. You bring down plenty of cash. The way I see it, you could use more." I figured I'd go right into the pitch. Let him at least hear me out before he got into whatever he was planning. "I got a connect that can get you product cheaper and more readily. That means you can sell more, and keep more profit. But it means that you need to tell your present supply to kick rocks. You understand?"

"You're offering me and my crew a change to make more money, right?"

I nodded.

He smiled. Then he reached into his pocket.

Quick as anything, Demus and I drew our guns and aimed at Stitch. Ozzie--bless his heart--was a few seconds behind, but eventually pulled his gun out too.

"Whoa! Whoa!" Stitch yelped, holding up his hands. "Calm down. I wasn't reaching for a gun." He paused. "May I?"

I repositioned myself to watch him closer and nodded. He reached in his pocket again and took out a Philly's blunt and a baggie of weed. He placed both on the counter and put his hands up again.

"I just figured we could smoke to the beginning of a new partnership."

Demus and I exchanged looks, silently asking, *Can you*

believe this motherfucker? After a moment, we turned back to Stitch, who still had his hands raised. We smiled and put our guns away.

"Yeah," I said, "roll it."

EASY AS IT went with Stitch, Rodney was another story altogether.

He still held a grudge. He didn't give any respect back, and gave Demus some shit for even coming onto his turf. I didn't mind, thinking he'd come around eventually. I had no problem waiting him out. It wasn't like I needed him. Shit would take a turn for him, business would go south, and he'd need a pick-me-up. I'd be willing to take his call when it finally came.

About two weeks after Demus tried to set a meet, things had turned. I managed to have Frog and Stitch do all they could to dry up his business. My beeper went off with a number I didn't recognize.

I called back from a payphone. "Yeah?"

"Rodney might wanna meet." I didn't recognize the voice.

"Who is this?"

"It's Burt. Rodney ain't too happy about business right now, but I think I might be able to get him to meet."

"Okay. Tonight."

I had him by the balls at that point. He just didn't know it yet. Not completely.

"Fuck, man, that's too soon." Burt sounded nervous.

"Tonight or never." I gave him an address to a vacant apartment and hung up.

I told Demus and Ozzie that we had plans that evening.

Demus smiled. "Rodney finally come around?"

"Maybe," I said. "Burt set it up. We'll see."

The three of us got to the vacant apartment well before Rodney and his crew were going to show. I made sure that besides Demus and Ozzie, there were at least four others hidden in the apartment, and another six nearby. I definitely didn't trust Rodney, especially now that he seemed desperate.

Even if he was willing to make a deal, he was going to rehash old grudges. I wasn't about to have that. I'd grown up and moved on. If he couldn't deal with the fact that some of the girls he was banging years ago gave up on him for me, that was his problem. It was petty bullshit, not something you let get in the way of doing real business. But here we were. Him acting like a whiny bitch, still all pissy because of some pussy.

I barely had the patience for it, but if I wanted to take full control of Richmond, I needed this meet. It was either going to work out or get him out of the way somehow. Burt was more of a pansy than Stitch turned out to be, but he might be able to hold things down, given an opportunity. Frog was doing pretty well for himself despite his own unlikable qualities.

As it grew closer to the time for the meet, I really hoped that Rodney had finally grown a pair and behaved like a man. He spent too much time thinking with his dick. That would prove to be his downfall, most likely.

The one and only positive thing I'll say about Rodney after this meet is that at least the fool had the smarts to show up on time. As far as anything else, he had everything coming to him that he got. As soon as he walked in the door, he was all about the same bitch that I stole from him. "You gonna make reparations?"

Rodney must have asked this four times two minutes into the meet. Burt kept him in check to some degree, which gave me hope that Burt might actually be able to get shit done on the street. At first, I tried to placate Rodney, still trying to make this business work.

"Yeah man, I'm trying to make some reparations."

I lowered myself for this man to try to keep things working, to keep things moving. I tried it once. But that was it.

When he asked for the third time, I was done. I wouldn't be doing business with Rodney. He was a waste of time, energy, and potential profits. His focus was on the wrong places.

In this business, you can't hold grudges. You acted and you moved on. If he had such an issue with me taking his girl, then he should have done something. But he didn't. Because he was a sucker. Still was. Years later and he's still huffing and puffing about this shit, causing him to miss out on a solid business opportunity.

No.

He needs to learn from his mistakes. He needs to learn to stop holding these long-ass grudges. A person who doesn't try to learn from their mistakes is a person you can't do business with.

We went through the motions a bit. I focused most of my attention on Burt. I gave him the same description I'd given the other crews in Richmond. But I was on edge. I needed to take care of this bullshit with Rodney without it appearing unprovoked. If he asked for his silly "reparations" one more time, that would be it. Otherwise, I'd let it slide and figure it out some other time.

"--so you're gonna see more profit because me and my man can move more product to you."

Burt was hooked, and I could tell Skinner--the third guy they brought--was being reeled in as well. Meanwhile, Rodney was fidgeting in his chair, anxious about something. "Yeah Jimmy, that's all well and good. I feel you, you know, it's a good offer...but you know, I still ain't heard shit about how my reparations over that thing."

I was hoping he said that.

I nodded at Demus.

Demus grabbed Rodney, hurled him to the floor, and then proceeded to hand him his reparations.

We stripped him. Every stitch of clothing he was wearing, we tore off. Demus pulled out some picture wire we used to string him up, tying his wrists behind his back then connected it to the wire we tied around his dick and balls. If he tugged with his arms, it would tighten the little noose around his genitals.

"Stay like that while us adults finish meeting. Whatever happens from here out is on you. How's that for reparations?"

Rodney whimpered, and nodded. He was chastened, and he was going to do whatever he could to make sure that he didn't lose his little Rodney in the process.

"You know, Burt," I said, "Rodney is likely gonna be out of commission for a while. I'm thinking that you're gonna be the guy to do business with."

I gave him a similar outline of the future as I did with Frog. I did this for two reasons: first, it was clear that after the embarrassment he suffered, Rodney wouldn't be running a crew much longer; second, I wanted Rodney to squirm.

And squirm he did.

By the end of the meet, Rodney was literally beside himself.

His frustration and anger got the better of him, making him forget his current predicament. By the time we left, he was scooping his genitals off the floor.

With that accomplished, I gained control over Richmond. I was the supplier. The top dog. My business was rocking, but I still needed to square things away elsewhere.

South Harrison Street and Berwyn Street in East Orange was the other place where I needed to get my product. There was a fairly large crew there, and they were working well. They were profitable, and the dope was getting out. But it wasn't my dope.

I had taken some of the major markets in New Jersey, but this hold out was important. It was where I was from. I couldn't let someone else control my own backyard, my own home.

I was on decent terms with Neville, the guy running the crew. There was a level of mutual respect. He ran a tight ship, which was good, and was a stand-up guy. Someone you could really appreciate in a lot of different ways. He was the go-to fellow for a lot of the guys in the neighborhood, and if he could, he'd help with whatever.

Neville usually hung out around 106 Harrison, a small apartment building. If you were looking for him or any of his top guys, you could usually find them on the stoop outside.

Riding high on my conquest of Richmond, I didn't bother sending Demus. I knew all of these guys. We went back. We might not have been completely tight, but we knew each other over the course of years growing up. Plus I'm sure Neville heard all about what went down in Richmond. In addition to my usual reputation, I was coasting, and relied on that to host the casual meeting I was hoping to have with him.

"Yo, Neville," I called out as I walked the block.

He stood up and met me halfway. "Oh shit, Jimmy!"

"You got a few minutes? I wanna run something by you."

"Shit yeah. Especially for you."

We walked toward the stoop. Dorkah, Scully, and Giant were there. They all nodded hello and went back to the card game they were playing.

"Private?" Neville asked.

"For now."

Neville nodded and motioned for his boys to scatter. "What's up?"

"Look Neville, I'm gonna cut right to the chase. I'm sure you heard about some movement down in VA, right?"

He nodded.

"I'm trying to cut you in on the same kind of deal here. I got a better supply, which means more and faster money. I wanna help you make more, while you help me. It's a win-win."

"But I heard about some of the other shit that went down in Richmond. I don't need trouble like that here."

"I came to you one-on-one Neville, because we've known each other. I'm not trying to make trouble. You know how important this neighborhood is to me, right?"

He nodded. "Yeah, I know it."

"I also know how much money is important to you. You're not stupid. More money and less hassle is a better day overall for you, right?"

"Right."

"That's why I'm making you this offer. You want a better day overall?"

He thought for a moment. "I do. I really do want a better day. But I gotta take care of the behind-the-scenes shit before I can take on your offer."

I smiled. "Neville, my man. Get whatever you need to get in order. Give me a reasonable date we can start working together, and I'll make sure whatever I gotta do is done before then."

We shook on it.

When you're untouchable, deals get made so much smoother.

15

HEADS UP

AFTER TAKING care of business in Richmond and New Jersey, I was riding high on the hog for a while. I was living the life of Riley. But I was being forced to network a little more. I needed to keep everything running smoothly on the streets, so I did what I had to do.

I'd throw on a pair of Clark's, Karl Kani jeans and a three-button polo, then head out on the town and land myself in a few different clubs to check on my subordinates. I preferred doing this at the clubs because, if I showed up on the streets, they'd want to know why. There would be confusion, questions. Most of all, there would be some kind of dog-and-pony show. Pulling up on them in the club though--when they've had a few drinks in them, loose, with their women and distracted by the feminine allure--was the perfect time to really see what's up.

There was one club in each area that I'd go to. If in Richmond, I'd go to Images on Hull Street. In Jersey, I'd be at Club Napoleon, over by East Orange High School. And in Brooklyn, I'd stop by the Biltmore Ballroom.

It wasn't normal to take a day off in this kind of business, but there were certain times of the year that I refused to do anything.

Not necessarily due to principle, but because I want those days to be the way I want them to be.

The most important of these days comes in late October.

This Scorpio takes his birthday off.

But it was not yet my birthday, so I was dressed and ready to head out. Since I was in Brooklyn, I'd be going to Biltmore that evening. I'd check in with some people, sit for a little while, perhaps have a Guinness Stout, then head home not long after. It was my last night of needing to be somewhere before my birthday, and I was looking forward to it.

At the bar, I was relaxing with a drink when this gorgeous specimen of a woman walked over and started flirting with me. I knew her from around the way, and was aware that she was with a fairly high-profile dude.

But I didn't see him around...

She told me to meet her in the bathroom as she left.

I excused myself from the few people I had been conversing with and headed toward the men's room. Girl had all but disappeared until I walked in. She poked her head out from one of the stall doors, then curled her finger to beckon me forward.

I did as instructed.

As soon as the stall door was closed and latched, she dropped to her knees, unzipped my pants, and pulled out my quickly hardening dick. It was in her mouth before I could do anything. Initially, I thought I'd be fucking her silly. I normally don't like getting my dick sucked, too many women don't know how to handle an uncircumcised man, but damn!

She went to town. She sucked on it like the world was

going to end if she didn't, as if this was what she had been born to accomplish. This was her holy grail.

She was an expert. She knew every right thing to do with her lips, her tongue, her teeth. She had no gag reflex and deep-throated me like it was nothing.

I was in heaven. This is how kings are supposed to be treated. I deserved it. I worked hard, and it was time to reap the rewards.

For a full thirty minutes, she sucked my dick like doing so would give her religious salvation. When she sensed me close to climax, she slowly stroked it, and told me to bust on her face.

She opened her mouth, stuck out her tongue, and looked up as I took it from her soft hands and aimed. The load sprayed all over. Up her nose, in her mouth, on her chin, in her eye; it went everywhere. She looked filthy, but all she did was smile and lick it off.

"Damn girl," was all I could manage.

The bathroom door flew open.

Her man walked in. "Bitch, you better not be in here. Dwayne seen you come in here."

I wasn't going to let him call this gorgeous, disgustingly filthy girl anything but her name, so I unlatched the door and let it slowly open. My dick was still out. She was still on her knees, trying to lick every last drop.

The boyfriend flew into a rage. He yelled and screamed and cursed, making no sense at all. But he was coming at me. I ducked as he swung a predictable punch, pulled out my .44 Llama, and slammed the butt of the pistol into his skull. There was an audible crunch.

He crumpled to the ground, which sobered up the girl from her dick high. She ran over to check on him, baby talking as he laid on the floor.

I calmly walked out the bathroom and exited the club,

ready to head home. I'd been out and about enough for one night. It was time for my own personal type of birthday celebration.

As soon as I walked in the door, I went to bed and crashed for an hour or so. When I woke up, it was early morning. The sun had not yet risen on the anniversary of my birth.

I threw on some clothes--comfortable shit that I liked to wear around the house--and sat down on my couch to start what was gonna be a nice, quiet day.

Until one thing ruined it.

The phone rang.

I didn't feel like answering. Most people knew not to bother me with wishes of a happy birthday, but there were always a few who wanted to do so. I figured it was early enough in the day for me to take the call, deal with the headache, and then have the rest of the day for myself.

It was a collect call.

I shook my head. Whatever it was couldn't be good. I accepted the charges. "Who the hell's calling me at this time of night?"

"Ah, mi mon, Curly."

That gave me pause.

A million things passed through my mind when hearing that name. Curly had been an associate, long ago. I almost forgot about him. We separated on bad terms after doing a lick together. I tried to keep tabs on him over the years, just to keep myself protected, but eventually he drifted off into obscurity and I no longer knew where he was, or what he was up to.

His problems were his problems. Wherever he found himself, he wasn't coming to look for me, and I certainly no longer needed him. I was at the top of my game making high dollar amounts. While most people might see $100k or $200k over a decade in their career, I was having that much cash pass through my hands in a day.

Maybe Curly called because he heard I was on the top. That certainly wouldn't have surprised me. The guy was a prime user. Not of drugs, but of those around him. He'd rob Peter to pay Paul, and have no problem working with you while shoving a knife into your back. Those bad terms were why we parted ways.

"My yout," I said. "How'd you get this number?"

"A mutual friend gave it to me. Only after I explained why and how serious it was that I contact you."

It was pointless to ask who the mutual friend was. Curly was calling from prison. There was a chance we weren't alone on the phone. I needed to be extra careful about what and how things were said, and the amount of time I spent on the line. The longer I stayed on the phone increased the chances of something coming up that I didn't want vocalized. It was second nature for me to be cautious. I wasn't going to slip up on the phone, but I still didn't trust Curly.

He claimed this was serious, but how serious?

Was it a business proposition? Did someone infiltrate my crew? Did he have information that he thought was serious? Or worse, was he trying to get out by having me talk about something?

"Look Jimmy, I understand you're reluctant to speak right now."

At least he wasn't fool enough to think I would keep talking and let the chips fall where they may.

"Your silence here is loud," Curly said. "I get it. So just hear me out."

"Uh-huh."

"Look, I'm solid, right. But some FBI special agents came to talk to me. They said if I wanted to help myself, I could help them. But I'm straight, right? They were asking about your crew. But mostly, the feds were asking about you and Demus. With Demus, I could tell they were fishing, trying to put two and two together. I didn't say anything. Maybe a little misdirection--"

I hung up right there.

Boy was running his mouth and it was liable to do nothing but land me in hot water. Probably nothing serious, but I don't want to deal with the feds, or even the local cops, at all.

Maybe I shouldn't have cut him off. Maybe I should have let him go on, get him to give up a little more information. But I didn't like what I was hearing.

I was frustrated.

If they were asking him about me, even just on a superficial level, it might have meant something more. But perhaps it meant nothing? My name came up, that's all. Just following a lead that won't pan out for them in the long run.

I left the house. Tasha would be back at some point, but I wanted to be alone.

Actually, no.

That's not true.

I wanted to call Demus. I knew we had to talk. But I didn't know what exactly needed to be discussed, or if I should even call him. If I did, it'd have to be from a payphone. Not a number they could find me at.

In order to calm myself, I drove over to the weed spot I liked in Franklin and Lincoln in Brooklyn. I bought myself some and got back in the car. It was late, dark, and peaceful as I sat there rolling my spliff.

I leaned back and lit it. Deeply inhaled the first hit, savoring the flavor and feel of the smoke. Then I replayed the conversation with Curly.

Is it possible they have something on me? Could I have slipped up so badly that I left some kind of trail?

I knew that I should fall back and lay low for a while. Let things blow over. But I had things lined up. Things in motion. A big score was planned with an even bigger pay off.

Mi haffi tek this juks, I thought.

It's just how it was. I couldn't let it go.

But after, I could lay low. Hop down to Richmond and take a cool off period. Coast on what I had put aside for a while.

But in my mind, an investigation--even the beginnings of one--is not an arrest. If I give them nothing to build a case on, that'll be just fine. But the feds are scandalous.

The feds could indict a ham sandwich for not having cheese.

It's not just that they're relentless, but they're also crooked. They'll keep after you just because they had you in their sights and didn't like the cut of your jib. Put simply, and as vulgarly as possible, once they get a hard on for you, they stroke until they've achieved the desired result.

I finished the spliff and tossed the roach. Putting the car in drive, I headed toward Atlantic Avenue, then into Manhattan to get to the Holland Tunnel. I needed to get to Jersey as quickly as I could.

I got to East Orange and headed over to Grove Street. Normally, I'd have stopped and checked in on business, but there was no time, nor a need at the moment. There was a small apartment I was renting on Grove Street. I parked the car out front and headed inside. It was nicely furnished and tricked out with lots of entertainment. It was cozy and I kept it just for me, almost never inviting visitors over. But that was not my real concern at the moment.

I rolled another spliff and grabbed a Guinness Stout from the fridge. I sat on the sofa, smoking and sipping, on edge.

Weed never made me paranoid, but I kept getting up to peek through the window blinds every ten minutes like clockwork.

I was being cautious.

I was not being paranoid.

Yet my mind often wandered back to the phone call, to something else Curly said before I hung up. *"They asked me about some murders they think you may have been involved with."*

That sentence played over and over in my head.

A drug charge was bad, but a murder charge is definitely no joking matter. You could potentially sit tight long enough to run out the clock on a drug charge, but that clock never stops for murder. For some shit that I didn't do, I'd be running forever. Or in prison forever.

I wondered what their angle was.

Why contact Curly? A chain is only as strong as its weakest link, and Curly definitely was a liability, but I hadn't spoken to him in years. He was not a part of this chain anymore. Hadn't been in a very long time. After all, we only did one job together.

What were the feds trying to do?

What was Curly trying to do?

What the fuck was I going to do?

As I sat on the couch wondering, the biggest concern I had revolved around whether or not Curly would remain solid. He was a piece of shit, of that there is no doubt. But in this situation, I could rely on him keeping quiet and not making things up to get a better deal.

He may have been opportunistic on the street, but it takes a lot for someone to turn snitch. Of course, there's a chance, Curly is looking at--or doing--a lot of time and wants to get out sooner than that. The carrot that the feds dangle in front of people can oftentimes be too much to brush aside, and even the best people can falter.

AFTER THE PHONE, I learned there legitimately was an investigation. I didn't know if Curly ever said anything to the feds or not, but ultimately, it would be years before the feds ever indicted and arrested me.

This didn't slow me down.

For better or worse, I threw caution to the wind and became a little more brazen in my activities. I followed the same mentality that a lot of people follow: they don't have shit on me, and they can't prove anything.

Let them investigate all they want, I thought. *Whatever comes of the investigation will be minimal, because I never let myself get directly connected to anything else.*

My focus was on my business, and at this point, it could run itself.

I was untouchable.

16

WAR

MY BIRTHDAY WAS OVER, and it had been ruined by Curly's phone call. All I wanted to do was sit back and relax by myself. Instead, I was dealing with the aftermath of the information he gave, faced with a million decisions that needed to be made.

There was no relaxation.

There was no rest.

All I had was half a spliff and a quarter of Guinness.

After some time passed, I began to fall back in the swing of things, getting life back to normal, and was no longer worried about this potential investigation. It was not my first waking thought, and I spent less time during the day wondering when the hammer would fall. I wasn't paranoid, but I was vigilant. There was no chance I'd stop thinking about the investigation completely--that was a sure-fire way to get caught--but I didn't need to focus all of my energy on it.

A few days after my birthday though, all hell broke loose.

I was driving around, killing some time, enjoying the music I was playing after just smoking a little. Everything was feeling alright. I turned the corner and my beeper started buzzing. I saw the number; it was urgent. I drove to where I knew I'd find Demus. "Jimmy, me and Ozzie was driving down by Lake Street when some dudes started shooting at us."

There was no preamble, no hello. Straight urgent business.

"The same dudes were selling weight on our block, down on Peach."

I knew precisely who he was talking about.

In my haste to conquer my territories, I never took care of a small faction that hustled on the corner of Peach and Lake. I assumed either they'd recognize how things were playing out and accept who was in charge, or that my guys running the area would take care of the smaller groups encroaching our territory. I was wrong.

Sometimes, you think small problems will just go away on their own, but more often than not, they become bigger, resulting in more time, energy, and effort to fix the issue. And right now, with this investigation, the last thing I needed was to solve a problem like this. But since Demus and Ozzie were involved in it, I couldn't leave it to my subordinates to handle. I needed to nip this issue in the bud, but I wanted to try a diplomatic approach.

Obviously, things had started off on the wrong foot.

Shooting at someone you're trying to work with--even though they were not trying to work with us--is probably a bad way to begin any negotiation. I would've loved to make an example out of one of these guys, show the neighborhood that there was no room for rival factions, but I needed to think with a clearer head.

The economics were obvious. My product was far better quality, but there were still hustlers who preferred to purchase cheaper in order to maximize their own profits. That was clearly what was going on.

The situation was volatile, so I called up some muscle for the sit down I'd set up. These guys were easy to hire as they enjoyed getting paid in cocaine, which I had a steady supply of, and they didn't have a problem following directions. Ears had big ears, Nose had a bulbous nose, Trigger pulled the trigger, Slim was rail thin, and Fats was large.

It was just how things were at the time. Lip service didn't exist back in the 80s and 90s. People weren't reinventing themselves every other month. You were who you were, and that was often defined early on in life. The handle you got was typically given to you when you were a kid, and that was what you were till the day you died. Didn't matter if Fats lost or gained weight. He got named Fats as a kid, and would be Fats even if he were a hundred pounds soaking wet as an adult.

These guys knew the score. If they agreed to help, they were in for the whole shebang.

There was an apartment down the way we could use. I told one of the hired hands that's where the sit down was going to be. All he needed to do was get the opposition's leader to show up. The rest of the hired hands were muscle to keep things under control. A strong show of force could keep things from escalating.

Demus, Ozzie, and I were in the apartment, waiting for the sit down to start. Ozzie believed, like I did, that this was the best move to make here. It would save headaches down the road. Demus, on the other hand, believed that swift and decisive action was the better course. Rather than sitting and talking, we should bring down the pain and move on.

Trouble was, I hadn't spoken to Demus about Curly's call yet. He wasn't privy to the information about a pending investigation. I needed to talk to him, but right then was not the time. He had just been shot at, was getting ready to play diplomat--which he hated--and there was no time to get down into the nitty-gritty of it. I didn't like leaving him in the dark, but there was little I could do.

Truth was, I really wanted this diplomatic angle to work out.

I'm not afraid of using violence to solve a problem, but only if it warrants it. This did not. Besides a few egos being bruised, no one was hurt during the shooting. If the issue could be ironed out and solved through a conversation, that was better all around.

Despite his protests, Demus was also loyal to a fault. He might disagree with me, and would probably voice his opinion later, but when I was set in the way I wanted to handle a situation, he went along and rolled with the punches. He was prepared for any eventuality, like I was.

Ozzie, on the other hand, was usually prepared for nothing other than people talking to each other. Though, I figured with the three of us and the extra help, the sit down would have order. This was far from the best laid plan, but it had a chance. The opposition were small-time gangbangers who wanted nothing to do with the plan.

While the three of us sat in the apartment waiting for them to show, Mario--one of the hired hands--was extending them the invitation. It was clear that it was going to take time for them to show up. Mikey, the shot caller of the opposition, usually kept himself pretty secluded. It was going to take a minute or two to get him the message.

So, we sat patiently.

Then we heard guns go off clear as day. We were only a few blocks from where Mikey holed himself up as the first shots were fired. We scrambled off the couch.

Ozzie ran to the shelter of the kitchen.

Demus went to the front door, gun in hand.

I had to hold him back, using every ounce of my strength to keep him from barreling out the door and into the fracas.

He looked at me very confused.

I shook my head and said nothing.

Demus understood something was up, but asked no further questions.

The neighborhood sounded like the middle of a Kuwait zone. If we ran out into the fight, we'd be done for. We could hold our own, but if there really was an investigation going on, police would be crawling around this neighborhood looking for anyone who might be involved. The last thing Demus and I needed was to be booked for just being in the area.

The gunfire was getting closer and closer to the apartment.

I didn't think that they were trying to get to the apartment itself, but there was a chance Mario told Mikey where we'd be. If that were the case, I knew I was a target. If you kill the king, you become the king, but my kingdom was not up for grabs. There were others ready and willing to step in and fill my shoes. Mikey may not understand this concept. Or he just thought it would be a big feather in his cap if he knocked off Jimmy.

No matter his thoughts, we were stuck. The gunfire was near. We could run into the street and try to disappear, but the FBI may already have APBs on us so local cops would know to pick us up. We were stymied there. We could stay put, but we'd be sitting ducks when Mikey and his boys arrived. We could put up a fight, but that would just lead to more legal problems in the future.

We hunkered down. Killed all the lights. I crawled over to one of the windows and looked out. There was an intense fight on the street. Two bodies laid on the ground. I wasn't sure if they were dead or just out of commission for the time being, but I could tell that one of them was Mario's guy.

It was a war zone as muzzle flashes lit up the dark street. Then sirens rang out. Blue and red lights brightened the area.

I breathed a sigh of relief.

Part of me wished, more than anything, to be down there, in the middle of that fight, but another part of me knew I'd have been done for one way or another if I did. Either dead or in cuffs. Demus was itching to get down there too, but as soon as he noticed the cops, he calmed down. We did not need to be hassled by the cops over this nonsense. Ozzie, still cowered in the kitchen. He had the smarts to run the business, but certainly not the physical prowess to command it.

There were shouts and yells coming from the street. The explosion of gunshots died. I shuffled to another window, trying to get a sense of what was going on. Several bodies were on the ground.

The police had swarmed and had at least two people in custody. Off in the distance, cops chased a few other people blocks down.

Demus, Ozzie and I made our way to the center of the room to figure out our next steps. We needed to get the hell out of Dodge. There was no expectation that the police were going to come looking for us, but we certainly didn't want to be spotted in the vicinity.

As we talked in hushed tones, I saw a flashlight sweep its way back and forth in the hallway outside the front door. The beam broke under the door of the apartment and made its way inside. I motioned for Demus and Ozzie to stay quiet.

No one approached the door, but in the quiet after the storm, I heard voices and the sounds of walkie-talkies out in the hallway.

We hurried to the window of the fire escape.

"This one here," a cop said.

Demus and I went out first.

By the time they busted down the door, Ozzie had finished getting through.

"Freeze!"

"Stop moving!"

"On the fire escape!"

We ran down three flights to the lowest level of the fire escape and made a beeline for its ladder. I dropped it. We all climbed down to the ground.

My car was a few blocks away, fortunately in the opposite direction of the battle's aftermath. Demus and Ozzie had a ride stashed somewhere else nearby. We split up and ran like the wind to try and get to our vehicles.

I got a few blocks away from the apartment and looked back. No one was chasing me, but I could just make out a small group of police in the alleyway where the fire escape let out, bunched together, looking in all directions.

I kept going, reached my car, and got in, quickly closing the door.

I didn't want to start the car just yet. The neighborhood was eerily quiet. The sound of an engine starting would have broken that silence.

So I sat. For a minute. Then five. A police car drove by. Then ten minutes.

After twenty minutes, I turned the key, started the car, and headed back to Brooklyn as the sky brightened from the rising morning sun, traffic already heavy on the streets.

I GOT HOME in time to watch the news coverage of the shooting. It was far worse than I thought. Several people, on both sides, were shot. Everyone got away and the police ultimately made no arrests.

The news showed images of various guns discarded in the street. The newscasters spoke on the caliber and types of weapons used, noting that the amount of firearms possessed by criminals often leaves the police outgunned. According to this report, however, one of the assailants was reportedly shot by police rather than rival shooters.

As I sat on my couch, taking all of that in, a recurring thought came back. I needed to get out of this drug shit. There is no longevity in it. The life span of the game is very short.

My new mantra: get out now.

My ringing telephone broke me out of the reverie.

I didn't want to talk to anyone. I was still longing for that quiet, lonely night I wished for on my birthday. I just kept dealing with one thing after another, navigating a shit storm of problems coming my way.

With a grunt, I pushed myself up off the couch and headed into the bedroom, grabbing the cordless phone from the nightstand.

"Yush," I curtly said.

"Rudebwoy," Demus replied.

"Yeah?"

"We need to make a statement. A real serious one. People need to remember who they're dealing with. They know what you're about, they know Jimmy Fyngaz, but you ain't made your presence felt on the streets in a long minute. This easy life you got set up for yourself with the drug income is all well and good, but you still gotta make yourself felt sometimes."

What Demus said had some truth to it. But the looming investigation also had to be considered. I still hadn't even had a conversation about it with Demus.

That's when I realized that this could be the perfect out for me, how I walked away from the drug game. I made money. I had respect. I didn't need to be this major player anymore. I could focus on the things I enjoyed, like spending more time on the juks. That was my real passion anyway.

If done right, my exit would be more powerful than anything else I could do. It would be felt, but also allow me to fade into obscurity. Exactly how I liked it.

"Demus, I hear you. I'll get back with you in a bit. Let's let things cool down real quick."

"Okay," he sighed--this was not the answer he wanted. "Link me."

***

ON A QUIET SUNDAY AFTERNOON, I drove my cashmere Acura LS to a gambling spot I frequented. It was outside my girl Jackie's place. She was like me: strong, forceful when necessary, and meticulous. She wasn't too hard on the eyes either, but I never found myself romantically interested. She handled her little gambling spot and made good money. I respected her, probably more than I respected most people.

As I pulled up to Jackie's I noticed that the wolves were out.

There was a group of people. Some gambling, some just hanging around. I brought my boy Mark with me. It had been awhile since he and I spent any time together, but I remembered how he liked to roll dice on occasion. Mostly, he liked to hang out and drink a bit. I'd known him since we were kids. We were almost polar opposites.

As Mark stepped out of the car after we parked a block away from Jackie's, I wondered how we stayed so close for so long. I opted for this criminal lifestyle, robbing and fighting and selling drugs, while he followed a straight and narrow path. He decided that kind of life was not for him early on. We were about the same age, but all of my varied experiences made me feel older than him. It made me feel paternal towards him. I loved him like a brother.

In that moment, I saw a life I might have lived if not for certain influences and choices, and a life I might be able to have--quiet, peaceful--once I walked away from the drug game.

We turned the corner toward Jackie's and were greeted by some very reputable fellows. I nodded in their direction and kept moving. They nodded back and returned to their conversations.

Mark went about his business--probably to find a drink--and I went about mine. I headed toward the ceelo game that was in full progress.

Everyone who was anyone was in this game. I recognized a lot in attendance just by the cars parked around the block, but the faces confirmed it. I saw the owners of the Twin Turbo Z, the Porsche, the BMW M3, the Typhoon Jeep, the Mustang 5.0, the Benz, and the Jaguar that were sitting on the block.

The Jaguar belonged to my sworn enemy, but that didn't matter here. Sunday was a day that we left the streets in the street. We took all grudges, petty or otherwise, and put them aside. Besides, everyone liked Jackie and the amenities of her gambling spot. No one wanted to be shunned because we got into some beef, as Jackie would send both parties packing and never let them come back.

We were not going to risk that kind of punishment. Not for anything. Jackie's spot was too important.

There had been a scene there a year before. It started over something small. Completely inconsequential. Most of us don't even remember--maybe a dice game, maybe someone's girl, maybe someone's taste in cars. Either way, two guys got into it.

There was a scuffle.

Fists were thrown.

It took Jackie all of about four seconds to get in the middle of the fight, break it up, and send the two offending fellows packing. Neither has been allowed back since. And both have tried. Several times. In fact, once in a while, one of them will show up, toting a gift they assumed Jackie might like, but she didn't want anything from them.

Jackie did not fuck around when it came to maintaining the peace at her place.

Regardless of the relative safety at Jackie's, I still carried. I had my Heckle & Koch 9mm tucked into the small of my back.

I wasn't worried about anything going down at the gambling spot, I was just cautious in general. Even though everyone--friends and foes alike--maintained decorum at Jackie's, there was always a chance someone would do something stupid.

I walked over to the dice game that was going on, watched for a moment, then turned to one of the guys waiting to roll. "What's the bank?"

"Ten thou," he answered. It was Koti. I'd seen him here before, and he was nothing if not cocky. Sometimes, it was deserved. Most times, it was not.

I turned to a young guy who was watching. "How much did he start with?" I nodded toward Koti.

"Only five hundred," the young guy said, "but he's been rolling good all day."

I would have loved to jump in the game and take him for a pretty penny, if for no other reason than to wipe that smug smile off his face.

I only brought a punk-ass $1500 with me. It wasn't enough to break the game, but it was enough to try my hand. Koti started with only $500. Maybe I could do the same. Keep rolling well and rake in the cash, especially from him.

I threw down a hundred after his next roll, hoping I'd get something out of the bet, but Koti rolled a headcrack, meaning he won the roll automatically. Fortune was not on my side. Without even touching the dice, I was already down hundred bucks.

The bet was so small, there was no reason for anyone to even look around to see who made it, let alone for anyone to start ribbing whoever had. We all tried to have a good time at Jackie's, so there was usually a lot of friendly joking around.

If someone made a huge bet and lost it all, they were the subject of some ridicule for a little while. If someone else rolled poorly, they too suffered verbally. But my hundred seemed insignificant at the moment.

I dropped two hundred on the next roll.

Koti, the chump that he is, rolled another six--another automatic win. I started to understand what the young dude meant when he said Koti was rolling good. I had barely been there a minute and was already out three hundred.

I looked up, briefly considering walking away with what was left in my pocket, and my eyes met Mark's.

He was sitting in the cut, drinking a Heineken, talking with some other guys. I don't know where he got the beer from, but I knew for sure it wasn't going to be his last. He raised the bottle in my direction, and I raised my hand back. He smiled--I was glad he was out having a good time. Then he turned back to his conversation, and I focused on the dice game.

I figured Koti couldn't be that lucky. He was bound to roll bad soon. I threw in five hundred on that belief. He rolled and the point was a five. Finally, there was a number I could shoot for. Nothing automatic.

The young guy next to me grabbed the dice and shook them in his hands, blowing on them between his thumbs. He tossed them, and as soon as they left his hands, he already knew he was fucked.

"Damn!" He shook his head.

The dice landed and stopped moving. It was an ace: Ike, Mike, and Spike. Automatic loser.

It was my turn to roll. I was happy he rolled a five. For some like myself, it was easy to beat. For whatever reason, I have real trouble beating a deuce. Someone throws a deuce, there's like a 95% chance I'm not going to beat it. But a five was my favorite point to roll. I was pumped. I was going to knock the arrogance off Koti's face and make a few dollars in the process.

As I shook the dice, I noticed a white MPV van drive down the block out of my periphery.

It was the second time I'd seen it, but didn't think much of it. As the day got later, finding parking around Jackie's got tougher and tougher. It was probably some guy coming to hang looking for a suitable place to throw their ride.

I was focused on throwing a five.

I crouched down and shook the dice one last time before I threw them.

The van's tires squealed and its engine roared as it made a U-turn and headed back down the block.

The next sound I heard was rapid gunfire. It was all around me. The onlookers and gamblers outside of Jackie's screamed and ran. Blood splattered everywhere, staining and dampening my clothes. It happened in no time at all.

I pulled out my gun and fired off a few shots at the van. The shooting stopped. The van's tires screeched as it peeled out.

I looked around when the coast was clear.

People had scattered. I was alone, except for the bodies of a few who had been shot. No one seemed to be moving. Broken glass, bloody money, and discarded lawn chairs--torn to shreds by the bullets--littered the street outside Jackie's house.

I was relieved when Jackie cautiously poked her head out

the glass shattered, bullet hole riddled front door of her home. I motioned for her to go back inside. She did.

I couldn't believe my luck. My life was saved because I crouched down to roll some dice. Most of the people around me, especially those standing behind the few of us shooting dice, took the brunt of the assault. Many had gotten away, but there were quite a few on the ground. I wasn't happy to see that other people, who appreciated Jackie's hospitality, were not as lucky.

As I surveyed the scene, I heard moaning coming from somewhere.

Someone survived.

I cautiously walked around the scene, listening. I looked at every body, trying to see if they were even alive. Then I realized the moaning was coming from the cut.

Where Mark had been sitting.

I found him lying on the ground. The front part of his forehead was caved in, and he was bleeding from his ears. He looked a mess, but in between the moans, he was saying something.

I leaned down to hear him.

"Grab the money. Get the money!" He kept repeating.

There was no way I was going to touch any of that money. It was covered in blood. I didn't need cash that badly.

I told Mark that everything was going to be alright, then made a bee-line to my car. On the way, I passed a small group of people.

"Call an ambulance," I said. "Someone back there really needs help."

One of them headed back toward Jackie's.

I jumped in my car and drove off.

It wasn't a matter of anything other than self-preservation.

I couldn't be mixed up in that. There was this pending investigation.

The last thing I needed for myself, just then, was to be involved in whatever was going on. Mark would understand that. I did what I could to make sure he was taken care of, and I was going to do one more thing.

I stopped at the first payphone I saw and called Mark's baby mom, Cindy. She answered on the third ring.

"Cindy. Brace yourself, okay? Mark's been shot. I need you to get to him."

She was in hysterics, but she managed to ask the only question that mattered. "Is he dead?"

"Last I saw him, he was alive. But he wasn't looking good. Get to him. There's an ambulance coming."

I hung up and got back in the car, jumped on the highway, then kept driving for a while.

TWO WEEKS LATER, I still couldn't stop thinking about what had happened.

Cindy got to the hospital and beeped me. When I called, she told me that the doctors had done emergency surgery on Mark. He was in very bad shape when he arrived, but fortunately, the doctors saved him. He was going to live. There was going to be permanent damage, but he should be able to make a recovery and return to a somewhat normal life.

I was ecstatic to hear that. I told Cindy to send Mark my love, and that I'd visit soon. In the meantime, I had something to do. I got into my car and headed out.

I had a goal in mind.

I noticed who was behind the wheel of the van that cruised

down the block, casing the place. It was part of the reason I ignored the van to begin with.

I pulled up in a halfway decent neighborhood. At the end of the block was a house I drove by three times to confirm the address. I parked down the block and walked up to the house. Stepped onto the porch. Flattened myself against the wall next to the front door. Knocked.

Feet shuffled inside and then the door opened.

As he was still looking straight ahead, I raised my gun and pointed it at his head. "Hello there."

He whimpered.

Cary B. Bowen
Stephen A. Bryant
Alexandra D. Bowen
Michael J. Champlin
D. Gregory Carr

Amy M. Curtis
Douglas A. Ramsour

LAW OFFICES OF
BOWEN, BRYANT, CHAMPLIN & CARR
1919 HUGUENOT ROAD, SUITE 300
RICHMOND, VIRGINIA 23235-4321

Phones (804) 379-1900
FAX (804) 370-5407

December 18, 1997

The Honorable Janet Reno
Attorney General of the United States
Main Justice Building
10th and Constitution Avenue, N.W.
Washington, D.C. 20530

Dear General Reno:

I received a copy of a letter to you from the Honorable Robert E. Payne of the U.S. District Court here in Richmond, Virginia. The thrust of Judge Payne's letter concerns a client that I, along with co-counsel, represented named Leonel Cazaco. Judge Payne's letter also refers to Cazaco's three co-defendants during an extremely lengthy and serious trial in Richmond last summer, which I am confident that you remember.

The issue of future dangerousness has usually left me somewhat perplexed and uneasy when it is either predicted for or against a particular individual. I think that though I am certainly not an expert in the area, I would consider all four of the defendants addressed by Judge Payne's letter as dangerous. I am confident that each of them would defend themselves if confronted with such a situation, and there was certainly evidence that they could be aggressive. I am not sure that after 20 years of representing people charged with criminal offenses in State and Federal Courts that I am in a position to predict who the most aggressive people are or who the most "future dangerous people are." I am often surprised and misled by appearances, reputations, etc.

I have no knowledge of any ███████████ between our client Cazaco and Dean Beckford though I am confident that there is a basis for Judge Payne's reference to the same. I have not received any information to that end so I am simply unable to comment. I am aware that Cazaco was never charged with such an offense.

During the mitigation phase after these four men were convicted of capital murder, there was evidence put on regarding the ADX institution in Colorado. There was also evidence that that is the most extreme custody that could be imposed on a prisoner and that because of the nature of the convictions that these four men would be considered for the same. As to Cazaco, at least, I do not believe that we ever told the jury during the penalty phase of our

The Honorable Janet Reno
Attorney General of the United States
December 17, 1997
Page 2

trial that he would be placed in the ADX facility or that he would be placed in any particular institution. Rather, we focused our evidence and our argument on how his upbringing and development facilitated him arriving at that juncture that we were at then in his life. I do not believe that we ever tried to lead the jury to believe that if they gave Cazaco a life sentence rather than a death sentence that he would spend the rest of his life at the ADX facility. I don't believe that we argued his future dangerousness at all. We simply argued that the death penalty was inappropriate. We did argue that a life sentence would not involve parole.

I am aware from some jury feedback that several of the jurors considered Cazaco the most dangerous of the defendants but that they also considered his mitigation evidence the most persuasive.

I write to you now only to try and balance what Judge Payne's perception was, not out of disrespect for Judge Payne, but out of respect for my duty to Cazaco. I am confident that I know extremely little about how the Bureau of Prisons classifies prisoners, and I am equally confident that that is an issue and an area that has been studied at length and developed by the Bureau of Prisons. I am also confident that Judge Payne's experience and reputation carries far more weight than mine, but I felt a need to express, as Cazaco's court appointed attorney, some opinion in mitigation of that expressed by Judge Payne. I hope that you will accept my comments in that light and will feel free to call me if you have questions or if I can be of any assistance.

Yours very truly,

Cary B. Bowen

CBB:dp
pc: Honorable Robert E. Payne, Judge
       United States District Court
       Robert J. Wagner, Esquire
       Gerald T. Zerkin, Esquire
       Elizabeth D. Scher, Esquire
       David P. Baugh, Esquire
       Reginald Barley, Esquire
       John C. Jones, Jr., Esquire
       Scott Brettschneider, Esquire
       Assistant United States Attorney David Novak
       Leonel Cazaco

17

____

INVESTIGATION

THERE IS no way to accurately describe how the investigation affected me. While I knew it was pending, and realized it would be coming, I tried to continue life as it normally was.

I didn't do anything outlandish out of concern that they were watching me closely.

I'd come to understand that this was a joint task force investigation: the FBI, the DEA, the state and the local police.

Despite that, I had no idea the magnitude of the investigation, or how far they would go in their efforts to nab the individuals they wanted to stick with RICO charges.

It was still early in this investigation, but not early enough that it wasn't my main focus.

I was on the couch, smoking a spliff and enjoying the indica, when Tasha beeped me. I looked at the pager and saw her phone number. I was focused on working out the details of what may have been the beginnings of a plan. I had no time for her right now.

She beeped me a second time. This time, she used her emergency code.

I shook my head. An emergency to her was certainly not an emergency to me. Least of all at that moment. I ignored it and returned to my thoughts.

What's their angle?

I couldn't quite get at that, but I had other lines of thought I was indulging. I had a stockpile of money set aside for lawyers and other associated fees. I worked, almost exclusively, with calculated risk. Part of that risk is planning for the worst. Never being caught unprepared.

Aside from lawyers and legal fees, part of the contingencies I considered included a bolt hole. For me, this was St. Kitts down in the Caribbean. I had ties to the island, and knew they did not have an extradition treaty with the United States. This was good. But it required me to be a citizen of St. Kitts to bene-fit. That was going to take a lot of planning and a large amount of luck to actually pull off. If I could make it happen--if all the stars aligned--I'd do it, but otherwise, I needed other plans in place too.

I filed this under the "Potential Solutions" column, as there was still quite a bit under the "Actual Problems." One of them being that I noticed one of my business partners made himself scarce since I notified him about the looming investigation. This gave me pause.

There may have been several reasons for his disappearance. They weren't all bad, but it still didn't sit right. I couldn't let myself get worked up about it, or else I'd start seeing FBI agents and enemies lurking in every shadow.

Another issue I had to deal with was helping Tasha get out from under her cousin's thumb by regaining custody of her child. She wholeheartedly believed every possible solution lay with me, and was adamant that I must make it happen. She understood the stress I was presently under with the investiga-tion, but she didn't seem patient enough to wait until I had things figured out. I appreciated her impatience--she was trying to get her own child back--but I was concerned she didn't appreciate my own dilemma.

There were still quite a few "Actual Problems" that I needed to consider and develop potential solutions for, but at the moment, figuring out what the police's angle was seemed most pressing. An escape would be an option--I had figured out a few possible angles--but I might not need one if I could get out from under the scrutiny of law enforcement. If I could blend back into the crowd, get off their radar, I wouldn't need a bolt hole. But I could only get out from under their thumb if I knew what their angle was.

I got up from the couch as I finished smoking. My thoughts were running in circles. I needed to take a break if I was going to get anywhere. I had some errands to run and some people to talk to, so I jumped in for a quick cold shower then headed out.

I was not looking forward to these chores. They involved visiting haunts I'd long since abandoned, and conversations with old disgruntled acquaintances. This was going to make for a very long night. But in order to move forward, to think through situations clearly, I needed to get this done.

I got in the car and started down Harrison Street in East Orange. I was headed to the Royal Inn Hotel. It was a jumping spot on the weekends and a lot of cats hung out there. There was a good chance I'd find the person I was looking for. Cautious as always, I parked a few blocks up, planning to walk all the way back to the hotel from there. No one needed to know where I was going, where my car was parked, or how to find me if I didn't want to be found.

However some plans don't work out the way you want them to.

As I parked, I noticed a Delta 88 slow down and move to the curb. In the rear-view mirror, I saw two guys in the car, trying their hardest to look inconspicuous. Acting like they were not looking at my car.

I wasn't about to stay and see what they wanted.

I was only two blocks away from the entrance to I-280, so I pulled away from the curb and jumped onto the highway, driving toward New York. As far as I could tell, the Delta 88 decided not to follow. I wasn't happy about the situation. I may have misread things.

But I was going to remain cautious.

———

"LOOK, Tasha, I got a lot on my plate right now. Give me some time to find out what's going on, and then I can deal with your situation. Okay?"

"When are you coming home?"

"Didn't you hear me? I got a lot of major shit going down right now. Besides, that ain't my home. I live wherever I lay my head down. You know that. Listen, I gotta run. I'll talk to you later."

I hung up, not knowing that later would be four months.

I probably should have taken her situation a little more seriously. I probably should have given it more consideration. Tasha had done a lot for me, and I'm sure the way I handled her situation may have been taken as a slap in the face. Eventually, I did keep my word by helping get her child back, and making Scully back off to leave her alone, but I'm pretty sure the way I handled things led directly to the deterioration of our relationship.

I didn't have the time, the energy, or focus to be with her. I kept my word and gave her the freedom she desired, so I considered our debt paid. I appreciated everything she had done for me, but I don't know if she ever appreciated what I did for her.

C'est la vie.

Thinking back, I realized that I hadn't heard from Demus in quite a while. I knew he was all right--I got that much from some mutual acquaintances--but otherwise, we both just never had a chance to really talk. Last we spoke, he mentioned hearing about a murder investigation in progress from a reliable source. While I did not doubt the veracity of murder being included, I had nothing to worry about from it, though there were still other things the cops could be looking into that would get me seriously jammed up. I had to remain vigilant to make sure I didn't fall into some trap.

It takes a lot to rock me, but I soon learned just how real the investigation was.

On the way to an associate's house, my pager went off. I didn't recognize the number, but attached to it was one of my personal codes. Figuring someone I knew may have gotten a new number, I found a payphone and called.

The phone rang and rang. I almost hung up when a recorded message clicked on. "You've reached the homicide department. No one is available to take your call at the moment..."

What the fuck!? I hung up immediately. *How the fuck did cops get my personal pager number?*

There were only a handful of people who had it, and there were even fewer who had that particular code. An emergency code that would make me drop everything to call back.

Fuck!

Someone's been compromised. That was the only thing I could think of. It was devastating news. If someone close to me was compromised, there were things they could talk about that I wouldn't want floating around.

I tried to think who it might be, but it didn't matter. Someone I knew, someone I was potentially close with, had turned on me. Loyalty was of paramount importance to me. I don't turn on people and I expect the same in return. But in this situation, I had to second-guess every action of everyone I knew. This threw off my ability to plan and make the right choices.

As much as that was a problem, it was manageable. I always screened my calls, so this was really no different. I called from a payphone, I saw who was on the other end, and I didn't say anything stupid on the phone.

Things took a more significant turn later.

I was driving back to New Jersey. Tailing me at a nice distance was a tan Toyota Sonata. It tried to appear inconspicuous, but after popping up in my rear view mirror over and over for dozens of miles, it was hard to miss.

I continued to drive as if I didn't notice it, but I was ready for anything. This could be it. I remained calm and drove at the same steady clip. Nothing strange.

The lights and siren turned on.

I pulled over to the side of the road. If necessary, I had a .44 Llama under the driver's seat, but I doubt it was going to come to that.

A few minutes went by.

What was going on? I wondered.

Maybe it was just a routine traffic stop. Maybe my left tail light had gone out. Maybe they were waiting for the tactical team to arrive in armored trucks and helicopters.

Finally, the passenger door of the Sonata opened and a detective stepped out. He swaggered over to my driver side and tapped on the window.

I rolled it down. "May I help you, officer?"

He looked at me for a moment. Glanced around the inside

of the car. Scanned me up and down. Then just stood, stock still, staring. "...You have your license, registration, and insurance?"

"Yes, of course." I started to reach for the glove box, but stopped short. He hasn't asked for them yet. I didn't want to make any sudden movements.

"Get them," he commanded, "and step to the back of the vehicle."

He walked to the rear of my car.

I got the appropriate paperwork from the glove box and slowly stepped out, gently closing the door.

"Any weapons or drugs in the car?"

"No, sir."

"Then you wouldn't mind me taking a look, right?" He headed toward the driver's side again.

"Actually, I would mind."

"Figured you'd say that." He came back. "See, I'll need one of two things to take a look: probable cause or a warrant. Since I don't have either, I'll just take a peek at your license. Don't move a muscle till I get back. Otherwise we might have some trouble with you resisting arrest, you follow?"

I stood there as he walked back to his car, chatted for a moment with the other cop, then came back with my license and paperwork. I was surprised at the quickness of it, but I knew there was nothing to be found if they ran my license.

"You're good to go," the detective said. "Be careful out there on the road."

"Thank you." I got back in my car and headed off.

I had no idea that the whole purpose of the stop was to produce a full-body picture of me--the most valuable thing they'd need for the investigation.

They clearly knew how and where to find me. They were either closely tracking me, or had someone who flipped telling them my whereabouts. Either way, it made life more difficult.

That difficulty wouldn't last long.

Shortly after the stop on the highway, I was driving through town, taking care of some loose ends and putting a few last-minute things in place. Contemplating things, I stopped at a red light on a fairly busy intersection.

In some ways, I understood how I reached this point where the feds were crawling up my back with an investigation looming. Much as I always tried to play things close to the vest and lay low, I was a known entity. It wasn't what I planned or worked for.

While waiting for the light to change, I leaned my head back, let out a deep sigh, and closed my eyes for a moment.

"JIMMY FINGERS! GET OUT OF THE CAR, NOW!"

The intersection was crowded with police cars.

There was little else I could do. They had planned and executed it well. I was stuck where I was.

I could have gotten out of the car and made a break for it. I could have tried to floor the accelerator and barreled through the police cars and take them on a high-speed chase. All these ideas flashed through my mind as I heard the shouted command.

"GET OUT OF THE CAR--SLOWLY--WITH YOUR HANDS IN THE AIR!"

I had a few seconds left. A few seconds to decide what to do.

Could I make it if I tried to run?

Probably not. I'm sure there were cops on foot all over the place.

What if I managed to get my car going?

No. Pretty unlikely I'd make it far.

I closed my eyes for a moment and took a deep breath.

My final breath as a free man.

WHILE THE INVESTIGATION itself may have been conducted in a manner outsiders considered ethical, it was only afterwards when I saw how fraught with holes the investigation truly was.

Shortly after my arrest, I was brought to the local police station and processed. This was nothing out of the ordinary. I was held pending my arraignment, but was required to stand in a line-up. I was placed among four other men who resembled me, if we were in an extremely dark locale and the person looking was legally blind. Despite this, I was not selected from the group line-up. Whomever the witness was, he or she did not seem to think I was the person who committed the crime I was suspected of.

My lawyer was ecstatic about this. I subsequently learned that the description of the person involved in this murder was nothing like my own physical appearance. The perpetrator was described, by eye-witnesses, as being below average height--approximately five-foot six to five-foot eight inches--and being of a heavy build, a stark contrast to my tall, fit body.

It seemed like I was going to walk out.

I was not identified, I did not fit the description, and I could place myself elsewhere during the time of the murder. Despite this, it didn't make one bit of difference. The police had other crimes they could have tied me up with, but were adamant about getting me for this murder.

There was overwhelming evidence to the contrary, including information supplied by one of the suspect's own family members, implicating him in the murder. Other suspects swore to police that I had nothing to do with it Evidence certainly existed showing I had amassed large quantities of and sold drugs, and there was probably ample evidence of me utilizing violence to keep people in check, but there existed not a single shred of evidence that spoke to me ever taking the life of another. This was painfully obvious to me, my attorneys, and even to the police officers and federal agents involved in this investigation.

Regardless, I was arrested, detained, and eventually indicted, tried, sentenced, and incarcerated for participating in murders I never even knew happened.

I could go on complaining about how the people involved in the investigation likely fucked me over and focused on a suspect who looked good on paper, instead of focusing on finding the real killer, but I'd sound like every other guy who got a bum rap from the feds.

I was not a good person when I was on the street. Selling drugs is wrong and destroys communities, yet I still did it. Violence does not always solve problems, yet I turned to it as a solution. I've done many things in my life, but I knew where to draw the line. Taking a life crosses it.

The police and federal agents didn't believe that of me. They saw a black kid from the streets, born elsewhere, making loads of money selling drugs, and assumed that murder was something I must be capable of.

This is despite the cooperating eye-witnesses, family members, victims, and piles of evidence that spoke to the contrary.

On paper, I looked like a phenomenal suspect. On paper, I looked every bit the guy who would do this. On paper, I must have appeared to them as a giant piece of shit. But in reality, I was the wrong guy.

If I am to be indicted, then indict me for the things that I did. But instead, all these cops wanted to clear their books of all the cold cases they couldn't solve. They weren't brilliant, and they most certainly weren't detectives. They were pencil-pushers who needed some convictions--high-profile convictions--to make them look good. The streets had labelled me a vicious criminal, and the police and federal government were prepared to wrongfully brand me a murderer.

PRIOR TO MY ARREST, I'd been trying to patch things up with Tasha before I helped take care of getting custody of her child. It had been a while since we spoke, but I wanted to touch base with her, as I was trying to wrap up loose ends in my life before anything happened with the pending investigation. I called her.

She answered on the second ring.

"Jimmy," she whined, "I'm worried. I haven't heard from you in forever, and no one seems to know where you are. Other people are looking for you too, and from what I hear, they're not finding you either."

I was baffled. I didn't imagine she knew anything about the investigation since I kept it under wraps. "Who else is looking for me?"

"Well," she hesitated, "I thought I was being followed a couple days back. My aunt told me some plainclothes detectives came around her house asking some questions about whether or not I lived there. Then, there was some dark blue car--a Delta 88, I think--with two white guys in it that I thought was following me. I mean, maybe I was being paranoid, but after--"

"Listen to me," I gruffly said. "How do you know they were looking for me? When they talked to you, what did they ask you?"

"Why are you assuming they talked to me? What makes you think that I'd even--"

"Tasha, it's obvious. What I'm trying to understand is why this wasn't the first thing you told me. You know this is important to me."

"I didn't say shit to them, okay, Jimmy? I didn't. They told me they could help me get custody of my son back."

"I told you I'd take care of that. You got my word. It'll be done. We'll talk soon."

That was the last conversation Tasha and I would ever have. Her behavior had become unacceptable. She was keeping things from me and acting in a way that made me suspicious. That was no good.

I kept my word. If there was anything that I am, it was a man of my word. I convinced Sully that it was in his best interest to leave Tasha alone and give her son back. There was no need for him to take care of the child for Tasha. She was an adult, well-situated with money, and could reasonably make sure that the needs of her own child were met. It took a bit of convincing, but over a period of time, he and I came to a mutual understanding regarding this particular issue.

But this still left me sitting and wondering where Demus was.

I hadn't heard from him in a bit of time. While the issue with Tasha had taken up some of my focus, I still wondered where my point-guy was.

I never once worried about Demus flipping. But his disappearance seemed odd. Demus knew how to lay low when necessary, but I wondered if him going deep underground was telling about what he heard on the streets.

I could try to source his whereabouts, but I didn't need to yet.

Let him lay low.

If something big was coming, he'd find a way to let me know. If not, he's just doing the right thing.

A few days later, my beeper went off. Hoping that it might be Demus, I looked, only to find it was two different associates letting me know about a money pickup. The code let me know where and when I could grab the cash.

As I was headed toward the pickup, I found myself wishing Demus was there. He was a solid guy, and I always appreciated having him by my side. At this point, I'm sure he knew the way the wind was blowing, and was doing his best to keep out of the breeze. He'd be tucked in tight somewhere, biding his time.

I should be doing the same thing, but I needed to keep getting money in order to fill out my rainy-day fund. A monsoon was coming, and I needed as much as I could get. Otherwise, the smart thing to do was head home, think things over, and start working on getting out of Dodge.

I pulled into a parking lot after circling the block for a while.

The pickup was just down the block at a house I regularly visited. Nothing was out of place when I glanced around. After a minute or so of reconnoitering, I got out of the car and headed to the house.

Everything was quiet.

The neighborhood, so often filled with noises, seemed eerily silent.

I knocked on the door.

An associate I knew let me in. We talked for a few minutes, smoking a joint in the kitchen, then he left to get the cash. It was a simple transaction I'd done dozens of times before. Nothing seemed off. Everything was perfectly commonplace.

I walked out carrying a small bag filled with twenties and fifties and hundreds, got back to my car, and drove off.

Everything was okay.

As I put some distance between myself and the pickup, I breathed a sigh of relief.

Since I'd been beeped, I grew concerned that something was going to happen at this pickup. I figured whoever in my crew may have been compromised was setting up an opportunity for the police to find, grab, and process me. I was relieved when I made it back into my car, and even more relieved when I made it home. No one had followed me, no one was waiting for me, there were no suspicious people or vehicles sitting in the lot when I parked.

I could relax.

I headed inside ready to kick off my shoes, sit my ass down on the couch, smoke a little ganja, and just rest my eyes.

It was going to be a nice ending to a very long day.

I went up to my apartment on the second floor, unaware of the black Pathfinder sitting down the block next to a hydrant. Unaware of the four guys sitting inside the vehicle. Unaware that my lock had been picked.

I missed everything.

The fact that my key didn't slide into the lock as smoothly as it usually does, requiring an extra jiggle to turn the lock that had newly made scratches on its face. I didn't notice the light in my apartment's front hallway being off, despite me always leaving it on. I only paid attention to the fact I just wanted to sit down and think.

My mind was on my next steps, looking into purchasing land in St. Kitts, a necessity in order to acquire citizenship. Citizenship down there meant no extradition. No extradition meant no more investigation.

This might be the right path to take.

I closed my front door.

The latch had barely clicked closed when the door was kicked open, nearly thrown off its hinges.

I rolled into my bedroom and grabbed the .44 Llama always under my pillow.

I heard voices from the other side of the apartment. They were talking in hushed tones to the people that just burst through my door.

Fuck!

How could I have not realized there were people in my apartment? That's some small-time sucker shit right there. How the fuck did I slip that badly?

The investigation had me all messed up. But it wasn't the cops that barged in. That was the good news. I could come out guns blazing.

The bad news was that some jackass thugs had found my place and broke in. This wasn't a random smash-and-grab kind of job. This was planned. These guys knew who they were going after and what was in store, yet they still took the risk.

I can hold my own in a fight. But six on one? All of whom are probably armed? There was no chance.

Where the fuck was Demus when I needed him?

Hell, I'd have even taken Ozzie. My only advantage was simply that I knew my apartment's layout better than anyone else.

Someone was approaching the bedroom.

I crawled toward the door. Took aim with the Llama as the assailant came around a corner. Fired a single shot directly at his kneecap.

He went down screaming.

Another assailant ran towards him to check on the commotion and got a bullet in the leg. He dropped, managing to get a few shots off in my direction. He missed, but shattered parts of the door.

I waited.

If they were going to keep coming, I was going to keep firing until I gained the upper hand.

No one else came around the corner, but I heard a muffled conversation from the other room, and watched as the two guys I shot crawled away.

"Yo, Jimmy!" A voice called.

I remained quiet.

"Yo, Jimmy, we know you in there. We ain't tryin' to off you. We got mad respect for you, but wit all this shit goin' on wit you right now, we ain't in no position to keep takin' orders from you." They paused. "Ya dig?"

This was a hostile take-over. These were guys who worked for me. They were attempting to exert dominance because they sensed blood in the water.

This fucking investigation was ruining everything.

Staying calm, I bided my time, hoping more of them would come around the corner. But the leader wasn't falling for the ruse.

"For real, Jimmy, we ain't tryin' to fuck you up. We just wanna talk. Figure some shit out."

I was considering whether or not to make my presence known and maybe, just maybe, talk to these motherfuckers when the sirens rang around my apartment.

A neighbor must have called the cops. Fortunately, my name wasn't on the lease for the apartment, nor were any of the rent payments traceable to me. The only items in the apartment that could identify me were on the bedside table.

There was a back way out of the apartment and building. I never rent a place that doesn't provide an alternative means of egress in an emergency. I grabbed my things from the nightstand and headed out the bedroom window.

If things worked out well, the assailants would still be shuffling out of the building when the cops showed up.

I made it back to my car and immediately felt safer. But that feeling was fleeting. Sure, I managed to escape the ambush, but my empire was in shambles. People were clamoring for my position, jockeying to be the top dog by taking Jimmy Fyngaz out of the picture. I needed to be on the ball. I couldn't afford to let my guard down. But more than that, I needed to make sure that everyone who worked with me understood this investigation was not affecting me in any way.

I was still in charge. I could still make decisions. And I was going to remain in that position permanently, no matter what.

My goals were clear, though the attack certainly muddied the waters as far as putting contingencies in place. Who could I trust now? Even more pertinent, where the fuck was Demus?

Laying low is one thing.

Being prepared for eventualities is another.

But an outright attack on our bread and butter? On our livelihood? That was something that needed to be answered for.

18

CLEAN UP

THE SHITSTORM at my apartment really threw me for a loop. Things were looking bad at the moment, and there was no way to paint a nicer picture. No rose-colored glasses to tint my world. No magic wand to wave my troubles away. I did my best to remain optimistic, but everything going on was making it difficult.

I safely made it back to another crash pad that I used on occasion. Caution was the word of the day from that point on, and I looked over my shoulder the entire time I drove there. I circled the block a dozen times. I checked the front hallway of the apartment building, then the back hallway, then the elevators, stairs, doors, vestibules.

Finally satisfied that no one was there, I went in. All I wanted to do was kick my feet up, close my eyes after having a little bit of the ganja, and relax. But there was no time for that.

I needed to think things through. I needed to figure things out. I needed to put things in their place. I needed to get things neatly and nicely tied up in a bow.

I wasn't planning on getting arrested, but I also wasn't going to leave anything to chance.

There were many loose ends to tie up, and many plans to lay down. The biggest problem was that I had no idea how much time I had to do all of this. I couldn't simply tell someone, "Hey, go take care of this for me."

"Yo, I need this done."

"Gimme that."

There was money to pick up, dealings to manipulate, people to talk to, plans to initiate.

I couldn't just abandon the business I started. I couldn't just leave people to fend for themselves. Doing so would end in one of two likely scenarios becoming reality. Either everyone I worked with would wither and die, or they'd wind up dead after a fight for power took place. I didn't want to see that happen.

I respected and cared for these people. I hand-picked them for their positions. I don't care to see needless loss of life.

Does it happen in my line of work?

Of course, and far too often, but never because of me. Throwing punches and kicks can put an errant situation back on track, but going beyond that doesn't do anything to get business done. It doesn't help make more money, and that's the goal: more money in my pocket.

I needed key people to know that I might be out of the picture for a little while. I needed my business in Virginia, New Jersey, and New York to thrive even when I was out of the picture. I needed cash to still make its way to me. I needed people to trust who would acknowledge that I was still in charge, even if not directly. I needed good people in good positions.

But that required me to get out of my crash pad and be out in public. After what just happened in my apartment, this was going to be significantly more difficult. I also needed to do some cleaning up. Stash some things and get rid of others.

First was wrapping everything up with Tasha. I told her I would, and I meant to keep my word. This was probably the easiest thing on my to-do list.

I paid a visit to her cousin's house, sat down with Scully, discussed Tasha's desire to be a mother to her son, and to not be held down by him any longer. There was a decent amount of posturing. A small altercation broke out. In the end, some money changed hands, and Tasha regained custody of her son.

If only everything else I needed to do was that easy.

Next was reaching out to some people I left behind long ago, people that I'd rather not be associated with anymore, but who I needed to wheel and deal with regardless. My old crew; Screw, Nic Nic and them.

Getting back in touch with them was a priority. Since they were also Jamaican, I knew they wouldn't snitch, but I still needed to touch base to make clear what may go down so they could watch their backs. While there was animosity between us because of how I left, I knew they would be receptive to the information I had to share.

My overly cautious brain, of course, didn't rule out that there was a possibility that they could turn.

We weren't on the islands anymore. This was the United States of America, Land of the Incarcerated. A country where all that had to be done was dangle jail time in front of someone to get them to turn on their own mother.

Someone had given the police my pager number and code. Only someone close to me could have received his information.

For all I knew, one of my old crew members could be sitting in the police's pocket. There wasn't much I could do to assure myself none of the old guys were informing. I had to go with my gut.

Just to be safe, I came up with an idea to keep their loyalty. A token gesture that would also solve another problem I had.

I needed to lighten the load of firearms that I possessed. I dumped a few of them in various places--trash cans, rivers, chucked out of the window of a car while I drove down the highway. But I kept a few of them.

A guy I knew had access to a smelter. He also knew another guy who made jewelry. I got my guy to take my .44 Llama--my most precious gun--and melt it down. From it, I had a few rings made.

These were going to be my offerings to my old and current friends, as well as anyone else I thought might need a reminder that I hadn't really gone anywhere, even if the worst happened. I wasn't sure how receptive the old crew would be to these gifts. They'd embrace me like the brother I was, no question. But underneath that façade, I wasn't sure if they were still holding a grudge.

I couldn't walk face them unprepared. Or alone.

I needed to find Demus.

Him being MIA was driving me crazy. I was beginning to question whether or not I had misplaced my trust. Laying low was one thing. Completely disappearing was another. For all I knew he was starting a new life somewhere in Witness Protection, getting ready to testify against me, giving information to the feds left and right.

I hated thinking this about him

Demus was my closest ally, but in situations like this, it can quickly become every man for himself. If that was his mindset, he may have dropped me completely, and such a thought left my mind wandering on the possibilities. Until I found Demus, talked to him, I'd keep doubting his loyalty.

While waiting on a good time to visit Screw, Nic Nic and them, I put some feelers out for Demus. He might be underground, but he was not in hiding. At least, I hoped not, as that would confirm my latest suspicions about him.

I first paged him myself. I stopped at a payphone a ways off from where I was staying, left my emergency code, then went to handle other business. I had to visit several places to gather a lot of cash.

The money was necessary for the final part of my plan--getting out of the country and into St. Kitts. No money meant no chance of travel. No chance of travel meant no freedom. And no freedom was not an option I was willing to consider.

There were five stash houses I visited throughout the day. I spent a bit of time at each one--smoked a little, shooting the breeze with the guys there--in order to make sure that these low-level crooks were content. A little face-time with the boss and they were pretty happy.

By the end of the day, I had a decent stockpile of cash, but hadn't heard back from Demus. We agreed, long ago, that in almost any situation, we would be available to the other. The fact that he didn't return my page rubbed me the wrong way.

It was still early in the evening, so I called Tom-Tom.

He answered on the second ring.

We chatted for a while, mostly catching up on old times and reminiscing. Then I got into the nitty-gritty about the investigation and what was going on with me. I trusted him. He was nowhere near the investigation, and would be so far off the feds' radar that he may never see a badge in person. After all of that, I got to the crux of my call. "You hear from Demus at all lately?"

There was a moment of hesitation before Tom-Tom answered. "Yeah. Yeah, I did. I'm not supposed to be telling people I did though."

I rolled my eyes. "He's not hiding from me. I know he's been laying low for a while, but I need to link him."

"He's trying to stay real incognito, man," Tom-Tom explained. "Besides, I don't even actually know where he is or how to directly get in touch. I know that you can call Spit. He probably knows a little more. That's where Demus called me from initially."

"I'll do that. You take care of yourself."

"You too, Jimmy. You need anything, just holler."

I hung up and pinched the bridge of my nose.

Motherfucker!

Looking for Demus was giving me a migraine. This was getting to be a real nuisance. I took a deep breath to center myself, then picked up the phone again and called Spit.

"Hello?" He answered.

"Yo, Spit, it's Jimmy."

"Jimmy! Holy shit! What's it been, a few years? Oh, man, there's so much to catch up on! How the hell are you? What have you been up to? You and Inez still going strong?"

I had no patience for small talk. "No. We're not together anymore. Listen, I'm actually calling to ask--"

"I'm so sorry to hear that you two aren't together anymore," he chimed in. "She was such a nice girl. You know, I was just thinking about her the other day--"

"Look, Spit, I'm in a bit of a rush. We can chat again real soon, but right now, I'm looking for Demus. I really need to link him, and Tom-Tom said I could get to him through you."

"So that's the only reason you called?" He whined.

"No! Of course not. I want to catch up. In fact, let's meet up for a bite to eat soon. But right now, I need to get in touch with Demus. It's business related."

"How's next Tuesday?"

"What?" I was confused. "For Demus?"

"No. For lunch. There's this great Caribbean place out my way. We could meet there. Have a leisurely lunch."

"Sure. Yeah. That's great." I would have agreed to nearly anything at that moment. "But right now, it's real important for me to get on the phone with Demus."

"All right."

He went silent.

"You still there?"

"Yeah, just hold on a second."

Hold on a second? Was Demus there? What the hell was he doing there? Spit was an okay guy, but hiding out with him would be a nightmare.

"Jimmy?" Spit said. "He's staying with Wayne. You know him?"

"Yeah, I know him. He's there now?"

"Should be," Spit said. "I talked to him yesterday."

"Okay. Thanks."

"And Jimmy, don't forget about lunch next--"

I hung up, happy the call was over, yet exhausted by this ridiculous run-around game of finding Demus.

Wayne's house wasn't off the beaten track, but it was a good place to lay low. I would have never thought to look for him there.

None of this helped with my anxiety about Demus at the moment. Everyone was fairly forthright about where and how I could get in touch with him, but was he really at Wayne's? If it were me, I'd tell people to feed someone else a line of bullshit about where and how to find me. But would Demus do that to me?

Despite my concerns, I took it as a good sign.

I had a lead.

I could finally look for Demus.

THERE WERE NO MORE phone calls.

No more last ditch attempts to merely get in touch.

It was time to talk to Demus face to face.

I hopped into my car and headed out. Wayne's place was in the boonies, but as I pulled onto a small dirt road that led up to his house, I spotted Demus's car. I sighed in relief. Then I got out and walked up to the small house, a one-bedroom that resembled a hunting cabin. There was no phone, barely any electricity, and running water. It was a quiet spot perfect for hiding and escaping from everything.

I stepped onto the porch.

Before I could even knock on the door, the click of a cocked gun sounded.

I threw my hands up, smiled, and turned to look at Demus, gun aimed at my head.

"You got me!" I laughed.

He kept the gun pointed at me.

"Why'd you come, Jimmy?" He asked. "I'm really trying to lay low."

"Fuck the lay low, and stop pointing that fucking gun at me. We got shit we need to discuss."

He glanced at the gun, then back to me. Despite my request, the gun remained up, but his wrist slackened a bit.

"Jimmy, I ain't trying to get caught up. I'm here, laying low, keeping my ears open, but my nose down, you got me?"

"Yeah, Demus, I got you. But, I'd get you a lot better if you put the shit down and we stepped inside. You feel me?"

Finally, he lowered the gun and opened the door.

We stepped into a small kitchen. There was a stove that looked like it hadn't been used in years with a hot plate on it. A small mini-fridge was plugged into an extension cord which ran out the window. Demus went straight for this and pulled out two Heinekens. He popped the caps off both and walked them over to the small table.

"What do you need, Jimmy?"

"Stow the attitude, yeah? I've been trying to warn you about this investigation, but we haven't had time to talk. First thing you hear about it, off you run. Explain that."

He looked at his feet. "Someone told me you already got caught up."

"And?"

"That's it."

"If l got caught up, why you need to go on the run?"

"Man, Jimmy, I dunno. So much shit was going on. There was all this shit running through my mind about what might happen, what could happen, what was gonna happen. I dunno. I just figured it was best to get the fuck out. Stay outta sight for a while. Maybe book it to better locales."

I shook my head. "Sometimes, you're a straight nincompoop. I've been paging you for days."

"No signal." He shrugged, then downed half his beer in one swig.

We sat there in silence for a moment.

"Look, Demus," I said, "they're investigating. They don't have shit, otherwise I'd have already been picked up. But they're trying to put shit together. I need to get back and talk to some people I used to deal with, but I don't trust them enough to go alone. I need you for that. But I also need you out and about with me. I need you to help me get things wrapped up for when it's time to hit the road. You feel me?"

He hesitated.

In all of the time I had known Demus, I had never seen him hesitate when I requested something of him, but I couldn't blame him. He had his own personal options to weigh, and was deeply considering what was best for him alone. Still, I knew who Demus was.

"If you weren't planning to help me out, you'd have headed down to the islands long before I got to this shithole. Think all you want on it, but you and I both know you're not gonna leave me high and dry."

He smiled.

I picked up my beer, clinked my glass against his, and took a long sip.

WE DROVE INTO BROOKLYN TOGETHER. We called up an old acquaintance of mine who agreed to let us crash for a night or two. Once we got there and settled in, I paged Screw using my code, hoping he would remember it. About an hour later, he paged me back. I excused myself and headed to a payphone down the block.

"Yo, Jimmy, my man, it's been a long time," Screw said. "To what do I owe this pleasure?"

"You got some time? We need to meet up and talk."

"We? You mean everyone, or just you and me?"

I sighed. You let someone think they're in charge, and it always goes to their head. "Whatever you think is best. I'm in town. Let me know where and when."

"Come by the old place, tonight. Ten?"

"Yeah, that's okay."

I walked away from the phone, slightly frustrated.

Screw was always a bit stuck up, thinking himself better than most. When we worked together, I cut him a lot of slack and got so used to the pretentiousness in his voice and mannerisms. But he was loyal and good at what he did. And I needed to talk with him and the others, make sure they knew about the investigation and to keep their mouths shut. I liked to believe they would all follow the standard Jamaican credo of zipping your lip, but they'd been Americanized. Nothing could be left to chance.

When I got back to the apartment, Demus laid out on the couch watching television. Once I explained what the plan was for that night, he agreed to play silent security. Neither of us thought anything violent was going to happen, but it was important to not show up alone.

I pulled out the rings I made from my pocket and handed it to Demus.

"What's this?" He asked.

"My Llama. Figured I'd give out tokens of appreciation to some people. Make sure no one forgets."

Demus rolled his eyes. "Now who's the nincompoop?"

I laughed.

Maybe he was right. But as Demus slipped the ring on, I could see the appreciation on his face as he admired it.

"I've got one for all of them too," I said. "A subtle reminder of who got them started, who made them money, and whose name to remember, but to keep out of their mouths."

"They're not gonna talk. It's sentimental as shit to give them a memento, but they're not gonna need a reminder to keep quiet."

"Doesn't hurt to try. Plus, I needed to do something with the gun. Seemed cool as hell."

Demus shook his head.

For the first time in our friendship, I wondered just how many times I've said or done something foolish in front of him, only for him to offer no judgment at all. I also wondered what it might mean now that he had. Perhaps I was becoming paranoid, or maybe just a little too conscious of my flaws. I decided not to focus on it. There were more important things to be done.

Once tonight was over, for better or for worse, I would have little else to worry about until the hammer fell.

We met up with Screw and the whole crew at an old apartment. So much time had passed, yet it still looked as if nothing changed. There was still the couch cushion with a mysterious dark stain on it and the old picture hanging on the wall. The place was the same as I remembered.

Screw let us in, and greeted both Demus and I warmly like we were old friends, as if we hadn't parted on bad terms. Immediately, we were suspicious. Screw offered us seats at the kitchen table. Everyone else was already there.

"Jimmy, what's going on?" Screw asked.

"Found myself in town and wanted to check in on you all," I said. "It's been a while."

"Check in on us?"

"Yeah."

Screw and the crew nodded. It was clear he was in charge. A position he always wanted. "This wouldn't have anything to do with--"

"I wanted to check in, because there's been some stuff going on in my life that may affect you."

I proceeded to explain to them the nature of the investigation, the things that had been going on in my life, and what my expectations were moving forward, not mentioning my concern of them talking, but implying that the police may come to chat.

They understood.

Screw had less and less to say as I continued talking. The others were rapt with attention. It was obvious they clearly still held respect for me, while Screw didn't. I knew that he had gathered everyone there with the intent of trying to knock me down a few pegs, but he was miserably unsuccessful.

The clincher--what sealed the deal and guaranteed everyone at the table would try to help me--was the rings. The stupid, sentimental rings. I gave one to each of them, Screw included, and explained how they'd been made.

"Wait, wait, wait--from that Llama?" Nic Nic asked. "The one you had all the way back then?"

I nodded.

Nic Nic looked at his ring with reverence.

Smiling, I threw a sideways glance at Demus. He just shook his head.

We left, amicably parting ways with everyone. Screw was not happy about how things had turned out, but he seemed congenial at the very least. I knew that his wheels were probably turning, trying to think of something to do that might hurt me somehow, but I also knew he was never going to say a word.

WITH THAT TAKEN CARE OF, all that was left was a quick stop at Ozzie's place to check on him. He was generally a liability, but could be counted on to clam up when necessary.

Demus and I headed back down toward Virginia.

We dropped by, unannounced, and spent a little bit of time with him, letting him know what might be going down, and what he needs to prepare himself for, in the event things got beyond my control. One can only guide things as much as the situation allows. After that, nature takes its course.

19

———————

LOW KEY

FOR BETTER OR WORSE, I did as much as I could to remove certain elements from my life during the investigation.

Some of my influences needed to go--they were bad for any continued success in the real world. Some of them needed to be left--mostly for their own benefit--the more time they spent around me, the worse off their own lives would be. I wanted to leave no unfinished business, which is why I spent so much time running around the east coast, wrapping up loose ends and working to put things in place to maintain business connections, income, and partnerships.

Loose ends were what, invariably, caught someone up. Forget to close out an account over here, leave a gun with prints lying around a stash house, or don't step in to say goodbye to that one guy who knew your dirty history; these are things that would take a man and bound him in chains for the rest of his days.

Like anything else, I was extremely methodical about how I took care of unfinished business and loose ends. Before bed each night, I reviewed the items on my To-Do list, seeing what was checked off and what was left to be done, prioritizing the most urgent issues.

At this time, I was renting a cozy, furnished room in Dover, New Jersey. It was next to impossible to connect me to this particular apartment, and unless the police had begun following me again--which they hadn't for some time--no one in the area knew me, my car, or anything. I was just some random guy renting an apartment.

My neighbors barely knew who I was since I kept to myself, but the few that I'd see would exchange pleasantries with me like anyone else. Suspicions were down, but I was also completely alone.

This was not wholly uncommon for me. I'm used to being alone. I can go days at a time without speaking to a single other person. I just needed some ganja, a bit of food, and a place to rest my head for a few hours. But the situation surrounding my need to be at this apartment made things feel different.

I cut everything and everyone out of my life. Not permanently, but certainly more than just for a little while. If I made a call, it could be traced and used against me, or used against whoever I was talking to leverage them against me.

I couldn't go to my old haunts.

I couldn't visit people.

I couldn't sit in a diner or a restaurant.

There were no wanted posters featuring my face hanging across the east coast, but I may run into someone, somewhere, and leave a faint enough trail for the cops to locate me. And if said person was already in hot water themselves, selling me out to save their own skin could prove too enticing. Needless to say, it was a risk I was unwilling to take.

Before I knew what was happening, nearly two weeks had gone by. Two solid weeks of loneliness and solitude in the apartment. Two solid weeks of no contact with other people.

Two solid weeks cooped up inside. It wasn't jail, but it was pretty close.

I liked the quiet, but this was getting to be too much. There's a limit to the amount of time a person can spend by themselves, and for me, it appeared to be two weeks. In most other circumstances, I would have figured something else out--some way to alleviate the boredom--but it was almost impossible to do anything without the potential of drawing unwanted attention. Even with those concerns, I wanted nothing more than to get out.

It was stupid to consider going anywhere. I should've just stayed put. There was no use risking freedom and safety just to take a drive, or walk around somewhere with nothing to do.

But my mind was made up.

I was going out.

I went into my closet, put on a black on black attire, then grabbed my 9mm Taurus, and headed out of the apartment.

Remaining inconspicuous tended to be easier in places like Dover, New Jersey. It was a small community made up of middle-class folks working regular jobs. This was a great place to lay low. No one was looking for a drug kingpin in a neighborhood like this. On the other hand, stepping out dressed how I was may have raised some alarms. Fortunately, most of the people in the neighborhood knew of me, and tended to look the other way.

There was still the question of getting out and doing something.

Dover was not the place for that. While it may have been a halfway decent place to remain under the radar, it was certainly not somewhere one went to have fun. For that, I needed to venture further from home, which was exactly what I wanted.

I drove my car onto the highway and cruised for a little while before coming to the exit for Morristown.

This was a larger town--a place where a fellow could get into a bit of trouble, if he was inclined that way. As it was, I wasn't looking for trouble, but a diversion that would occupy me for an hour or two. Something to help shake loose the cobwebs that formed over the last two weeks.

Unbeknownst to me, Morristown had a Caribbean population big enough to warrant a Jamaican restaurant. It was small and easy to miss, as it was tucked in among several other eateries like pizzarias, sandwich shops, and diners. I felt like it was fate.

As I walked to the storefront after parking the car, I scoped out my surroundings. Two weeks of solitude had not lessened my caution. I still looked over every car, into every window, and around every corner. I double-checked to make sure my gun was where it was supposed to be, then headed inside the restaurant.

A nice looking woman stood at the counter. She smiled as I approached, ready to take an order.

"Mawnin," I said.

"Mornin'," she replied. "What can I get 'cha?"

"Give me a plate of liver and dumplings and a peanut punch."

She nodded, as if she approved my order, then wrote it down. "You gonna stay here or is it gonna be to go?"

I looked around.

The place seemed fairly empty and had a nice vibe. It felt comfortable, homey; definitely more welcoming than the prison cell my apartment had become. The woman was also very pleasant to look at, and even if we said nothing else to each other, she'd be very nice company indeed.

"I'll be eatin' here," I said.

"Grab a table--anywhere's good," she said. "When your food's ready, I'll bring it over."

She walked over to the kitchen window and passed over my order while I went to the table furthest from the doors and windows, but close enough for me to see everything that was going on inside and out. My back was toward the cute cashier, but I got a decent enough reflection of her in the window. She considered me with an intense look of curiosity, but it didn't strike me as suspicious.

Any other time, I would have tried to pick her up, flirting like mad with this girl. She had many attractive qualities. A cute face, a stunning smile, and shapeliness that gave her a bottom-heavy build that I loved. All of it contributed to a very nice package, and if I didn't have a billion things going on, I'd already have her out the restaurant and in my car. But that was for another time and place.

I was deep in thought when she walked over to my table and set my food down. For a moment, she stood there, just looking at me. Then she cleared her throat.

I looked up and smiled in recognition. "Thanks."

With a smirk, she walked back to her perch behind the cash register.

My stomach rumbled. I was hungry. The food smelled incredible, and looked even better.

I was about to dig in when I noticed a few other people now in the restaurant.

How could I have missed them coming in?

Maybe I had lost my touch. Normally, nothing like that would have gotten past me, yet two tables were occupied by people I didn't detect come in.

I couldn't believe I'd been so unfocused. I took a bite of the meal and cautiously looked around, assessing who was there.

At one table was a lovesick young couple, clearly on a date. Sat at the second table next to me was--

"So, your hideaway isn't as secluded as you wanted it to be."

Demus!

He smugly smiled at me. In spite of being dumbstruck, a part of me wanted to wipe that look off his face.

"Suppose not," I replied.

"I was passing through and decided to check on you. Been waiting two weeks for you to come out of your cubby hole."

"Two weeks?!" I was incredulous. "Why you been waiting that long?"

"You act like I was spying on you. You know that ain't the case." Demus leaned back in his chair, grinning. "It was you, after all, who got me outta my own bolt hole to play your game. Figured I'd turn the tables and pay ya back."

"What's the occasion?" I turned closer to him. "We concluded all of our business affairs. So, what now?"

"It's true, my man, we have concluded all of our affairs, but not all of our business has been concluded."

I nodded, slumped in my seat, then pulled out my gun and pointed it right at Demus's stomach under the table.

I thought back on everything we had done together. Not just the jobs and licks, but the times we just sat back to enjoy some food, talk about life, smoke a spliff, drink a beer. The most significant memory though, was one of our latest interactions. When Demus held a gun to my head, even after I repeatedly told him to stand down.

He was a good soldier, a loyal ally, but times were changing. And as times changed, so too did attitudes. A friend a minute ago might be waiting patiently to stab your back the next.

The rules changed as soon as the police started this bogus investigation. Relationships were torn apart. Loyalty went out the window for some. For me, it was a luxury I could no longer afford.

In my line of work, I could never truly trust anyone, not completely. It came with the territory. If I gave someone so much as an inch, they were likely to take a mile and leave me behind.

I couldn't do that to myself, so I sat in that small Jamaican restaurant, aiming a gun at the one person who came closest to earning my complete trust. Any feelings of sentimentality were overrode by my instincts. I had a clean shot, and if the need arose, I wouldn't have hesitated to take him out.

But why was he here?

Yes, I searched him out when he was in his hidey-hole, trying to lay low, but that was to warn him. Keep him safe. Was he here for the same reasons, or something else?

My insides were tearing me apart. I just wanted to leave the apartment and have a decent meal. Even that was ruined. I wanted to punch a hole in the table. I was boiling with anger. "Okay, what's so important that you came all the way here to pay me this unannounced visit?"

"Jimmy, there are some associates I'm not too sure of. Some of the information floating around out there could have only come from someone close. Someone in the inner circle. I think Ozzie and maybe one other--"

"That's it?" I asked. "I've already considered that. Everything has gone to shit and nothing is clear cut anymore. I'm feeling my way through it, flying by the seat of my pants."

I was a bit relieved. Not enough to rethink my current thoughts on him, but enough to ease my finger off the trigger and put the gun away before Demus could notice. I stood up from the table.

With cat-like agility, Demus did the same.

We stood there for a while, neither of us uttering a word for what felt like hours.

Finally, I looked at Demus. "Look, I hope all the business is done for now. Let's part as friends."

He nodded. "As friends."

"However this plays out, Demus, I wish you the best."

"Likewise, Jimmy, likewise."

I turned and walked out the door of the restaurant without looking back; it was the end of a chapter.

I got in my car and headed to New York, replaying the conversation with Demus in my head. Something seemed off. It had little to do with the fact that the Dover apartment was compromised, though it did annoy me how Demus found it fairly quickly when no one else had known about the place.

Something else bothered me.

What Demus said about our associates. It was as if he knew something that I didn't. He mentioned "one other" who might be ratting. Who? I checked on everyone close to us. They were all dead ends. No one seemed to have a connection to the police, but that didn't mean that was true.

Either way, Demus had become a bit of a liability. With the police likely tracking both of us, it was not a good idea to be seen together. Even if he was squeaky clean, it was better for the both of us to separate. I'd done all I could to warn him, and he did all he could for me. Whatever the consequence, whatever the consideration, whatever was interfering with my continued freedom needed to be dealt with. And I could not show an ounce of leniency.

I finally reached Brooklyn and parked the car outside the apartment building on Utica and Union, straight across from Lincoln Terrace Park. I took a deep breath as I stepped out of the car, savoring the refreshing New York City air. It felt great to be back in a familiar area.

Brooklyn was home.

I felt comfortable there. Happy there. Sure, there were plenty of bad memories, plenty of times I'd be glad to forget, but Brooklyn was my first taste of the United States. I'll never forget it, and it will never leave me. The old saying, you can take the boy out of Brooklyn, but you can't take Brooklyn out of the boy, never felt more true as my feet touched the concrete. I sighed in satisfaction. Brooklyn just felt right.

Once done reminiscing, I entered the building. As far as I knew, I arrived undetected. I figured that I might have a little bit of time before someone noticed me. My car was a clear give-away that I was in town, and there were going to be some faces around the neighborhood who'd recognize me. For now, I needed to get inside to gather some belongings. This was not going to be a long reunion trip. Simply a quick nostalgia tour before hopping back on the road.

I knocked on the door.

No response.

After pounding on it for the third time, it opened with a click. I had no time for words. I pushed my way inside and headed straight for a back bedroom. I had a stash built into the floorboards under the bedroom carpet. I lifted the corner of the carpet and pried up a loose board, revealing a metal box. I poured its contents into a duffel bag I carried, sealed it up, then got up to leave.

Everything appeared in order.

As I headed to the door, my associate said, "Demus stopped by. He didn't say why or stay."

Shit!

"Of course he did," I said.

I was seething as I left. Demus said nothing about this, and that alone was suspicious. There was little I could do, so I took the building's back exit, going all the way down to the trash strewn basement and forced my way through the side door, partially blocked by a rusted shopping cart. By this point, it was likely that someone had spotted my car, or spotted me going into the building despite my caution.

I shouldn't have driven that car into the city, I thought.

But after my conversation with Demus, I needed to reach Brooklyn as fast as possible. I had no time to change wheels.

I looked around the corner of the building before exposing myself to whatever might be out there. Though still angry, I needed to remember to keep a level head, think things through before taking action. I was liable to make mistakes while this angry, and I couldn't afford any more.

The coast appeared to be clear. I jogged to my car with the duffel bag slung over my shoulder, checked once more, then got in.

As soon as I closed the door, lights and sirens blared on.

The cops forcibly removed me from the car, threw me to the ground, then locked me in cuffs. I was in a daze as they Mirandized and dragged me to a police car, pushing my head down to shove me into the back seat. I sat silently in the back of the police car for what felt like days as they drove me to the nearest precinct where I was promptly interviewed.

I almost laughed at how ridiculous it all seemed.

We sat in a cinderblock room. I was in a metal chair, handcuffs running through an eye-bolt welded to a metal table bolted to the floor. As much as I moved and flailed about, the table never budged. Two detectives sat across from me. One had a mustache and sipped steaming coffee from a blue paper cup, the beverage carrying an aroma that both whetted my appetite and nauseated me. After a few more sips, Mustache asked if I wanted some.

I declined.

Mustache asked if I wanted something to eat.

I declined.

Then Mustache asked if I wanted a cigarette, or something to make me more comfortable.

I declined.

The other cop pulled a cigarette out of his pocket and lit it, chewing on the smoke as he savored each hit like it was the last cigarette on the planet. It was disgusting to watch. Yet I continued to look at him, determined not to give him the satisfaction of beating me in a staring contest.

Mustache and Cigarette talked for a while. They spent much of it discussing the $25,000 in the duffel, as well as a pair of handcuffs and a stun gun. My focus was on the fact they hadn't yet mentioned the gun underneath my car's passenger seat. They either hadn't found it, or were working their way around to bringing it up, trying to catch me off guard.

That was not going to happen.

Mustache led the conversation, with Cigarette, occasionally, tossing in his two cents.

Half-a-pack into our discussion, Cigarette took the lead and started asking me about some alleged murders. "You're the prime suspect." They supposedly had a ton of evidence proving it was me. Through a mouthful of smoke, he let me know that, "We have you, dead to rights, no chance of you walking out of here."

When his tirade was over--which required another three cigarettes for him to get through--he sat down, smug and satisfied, blowing smoke out of his nostrils.

I sat back in my chair, waiting for more.

Nothing came.

It was the first time, in probably an hour, that the room was completely silent.

"What do you have to say to all that?" a grinning Cigarette asked.

"Lawyer."

"What?" Mustache said, feigning deafness.

"Lawyer."

Mustache sucked his teeth. Cigarette just nodded. They rose from their respective chairs and left.

I was alone.

Livid.

There was nothing I could do about it, so I sat and seethed. Later, Mustache returned by himself and unshackled me.

As we walked from the room, he explained, "We're booking you for the robbery implements we found in your vehicle."

I chuckled to myself. So much for not walking out of there for being caught dead to rights. It was a bullshit charge meant to try and intimidate me. They were going to have to do better.

After the cops obtained my fingerprints, I was driven to Central Booking--a tomb-like place under the Kings County Criminal court building--to be arraigned later that day. In total, I spent a total of six hours there and at the local precinct. The judge that heard my case granted me a $100,000 bail, and after posting 10% of that, I was able to walk out of the courthouse. All that was left was to retrieve my car--which I'd been told was ready to be released back once I paid the impound fees.

Despite being detained, the process of walking out free was smooth sailing. It should've put me at ease. Yet all I felt was confusion and concern when trying to understand the latest mystery my mind kept inevitably wandering to.

There was no gun in my car. It seemed they hadn't found it, which meant it was either going to bite me in the ass later, or it wasn't there at all. But if not there, then where?

20
____

BLUNDER

THE ERA of hustling and juks was winding down, and it seemed like there was little I could do about it.

My best move was to go back to doing what I knew. Stop laying low, as doing so did nothing for me. When I sat back, waiting to see how the universe unfolded, things kept playing out in a way I wasn't happy about. Without my fingers in the mix, the end result would be the same. Hiding out was not a good look.

It was time to return to my craft.

I spent a lot of time thinking about what Demus said at our last meeting. A lot of it didn't sit right with me. Tons of questions had been raised and no one could provide answers. Notably, the missing gun plagued my thoughts.

Where was it?

If the cops had it, they wouldn't have made it so easy for me to walk.

But if they didn't have it, who did?

My thoughts came back to Demus.

I considered our chance meeting years ago at that robbery.

The stairwell standoff that solidified our relationship and formed a rock-solid partnership. Was our random meeting in Dover by chance too?

He was no one's fool; he was always on the ball and played the game well. I think he came to realize that I was on to him. What I had always thought came naturally to him, his innate sense of loyalty and his willingness to do what it takes to protect others, began to seem like a highly crafted skill, honed over years of practice.

Demus was like me in many ways: a survivor, always ready to roll and willing to take a hit. But that's where the similarities ended. Unlike him, there were things that I was principal-bound to. I firmly believed that loyalty and trust were as sacred as life itself. It went beyond disrespect to be disloyal to some-one--it bordered on mortal sin. There was never a reason to drop your loyalties to someone who had not done you wrong. Only people who turned on you deserved such a fate.

That's when I realized all of my thoughts were taking me to one specific decision. A drastic decision. An enormous, gigan-tic, Titanic risk.

All my life, I believed risks were worth taking, but it was important to be calculated. I embraced the ultimate outcome, death, as if it were my lover. Every risk I took could lead me to Death's arms. It is the inevitability of life.

Rather than fearing it, I embraced death, welcomed it, giving myself the ability to go about my business and life without fear of this outcome. I looked at death as a step that I would one day take. But if I looked at my risks and calculated the likelihood of whether or not I'd face death, it made making decisions simpler.

This risk I was currently contemplating was incalculable.

There were variables and elements that I had absolutely no way of foreseeing. Try as I might, no line of thinking could solidify the odds of each outcome, which turned it into a crap shoot.

Still, I had no choice but to do it.

The upside was simply that, for whatever happened in the end, all of the inconsistencies and curiosities, the concerns and questions, everything would be solved.

My life was rapidly turning upside-down. I was losing my hold on things that I held firmly for years. Loyalties were wafting away on the slightest of breezes. Enemies were circling. The idea that merely getting answers was a sufficient reason to take a life-or-death risk would've been crazy if I led a regular lifestyle. But this was far from everyday life.

Nothing I learned or discovered in the next few days was going to stop the freight train of this investigation from barreling down on me, but at least it would put some things in proper context. If I was going down, I wanted to go down knowing who fucked me over. I needed to know who remained on my side and who didn't. Trust, being of paramount importance to me, needed to be something I could keep tabs on. I didn't want to continue trusting in someone that no longer deserved it, nor did I want to pull my trust from someone who remained loyal to me throughout the entire ordeal.

In order to figure this out, I needed answers.

I grabbed my car keys and left the apartment. I knew there were dozens of things that were out of my control and line of sight, but this was a piece of business that needed to be taken care of, and should have been taken care of as soon as I heard about the investigation. I waited long enough. Better late than never.

I PULLED up to an apartment complex that afternoon. It was a place that many of my business associates frequented. There was no guarantee that anyone would be around, let alone the person I was specifically looking for. But I needed to give it a shot.

If he was here, I'd be able to take care of this business quickly. If he wasn't, it meant a lot more driving, looking, and talking around. I didn't want that. I preferred simplicity.

Thankfully, the man was a creature of habit, and I knew his habits well.

No sooner did I put my foot on the ground when stepping out of my car did my beeper go off. I looked at it. Staring me in the face was Ozzie's code.

Dude must have a sixth sense, I thought.

I paused for a moment, pondering the coincidental timing of the page. It didn't change my mind. This business needed to be addressed, no matter what.

Too much was going on in my life, in the investigation, and with people I knew. I would not veer or run away from the course I set. I had to see this through.

I entered the building and headed for apartment 3D, hustling up the staircase three steps at a time. When reaching the third floor, I hoped that Ozzie was there alone. I didn't want to deal with anyone else.

Ozzie beeped me again, unaware that I was right outside his door. Or did he? I eased my gun out, placed the toe of my Timberland boot against the inside frame of the door--ready to slip my foot in to jam it--and knocked.

I braced myself when hearing the thuds of footsteps.

The peephole flipped open. I saw Ozzie's eye. He exhaled deeply once seeing me.

I didn't put the gun away. Although he was a friendly face,

with everything going on, I needed to be cautious. Friendly or not, this could be the last face I saw.

He unchained the door and turned the knob. I pushed myself through the door and grabbed him by the throat, then kicked the door closed once inside, jamming the gun hard into his side.

The utter shock on his face was real.

I pressed him against the wall, my hand squeezing his windpipe while the barrel of my gun pressed directly into his liver.

All of this force was necessary. There was no other way. I took no comfort in doing this to a once-trusted business partner.

"Jimmy," Ozzie wheezed, "Jimmy, what the fuck?"

"No questions," I whispered, " just answers." I glanced down the hallway. "How many here with you?"

"It's just me," he rasped.

I relaxed my grip on his throat. "I'm gonna ask you some stuff, and I need you to be straight with me. This is not the time for bullshit. Do you understand?"

He nodded. I could feel his breath. His eyes kept flicking toward the gun.

"Don't worry about the gun," I said. "You answer my questions honestly and quickly, and it'll be like it isn't there."

"O-okay," he stammered. "What-what do you wanna know?"

"I wanna know it all. I wanna know everything that matters, ya dig?"

On the verge of tears, he gulped for air as he spoke. "Uh-huh. They came by. They talked to me."

This didn't surprise me, though I felt a little worse about my current situation.

"I figured as much, Ozzie. But that's not all."

"Nuh-no. They asked me stuff. They told me they knew

things. They just--they just wanted me to--to fill in blanks. B-but I said nothing. Duh-Duh-Demus told me they might come. He s-s-said there might be questions. But--but I didn't talk, Jimmy. I d-d-didn't say anything."

Ozzie was blubbering.

It was horrible to watch. I liked him. Ozzie was a decent guy. I was fairly certain he hadn't said anything, but one could never be quite sure.

"What questions did they have?"

"They asked about R-R-Richmond. Some robberies there. They couldn't connect you to them. And a guh-gun. I told them nothing."

Ozzie was calming down, breath returning to normal.

"They talked to you a few days ago," I said. "That's the information I got. Why'd you only first beep me today? Why not three days ago?"

He shrugged. "I needed to make sure that I was secure on my end first."

I pistol-whipped Ozzie across the ear. A trickle of blood leaked out. As he reached for the wound, I stepped back, letting him fall to the ground. Gun still held against him, I silently dared him to move.

He didn't.

Ozzie stayed on the floor, curled up in the fetal position, holding his ear, whimpering.

"Let's try this again." I pulled out the fishing line I carried with me and dangled it so he could see it.

He held up his hands in protest. "No! Jimmy, I told them nothing!"

I kicked him in the stomach and he wet himself. I hated doing that to him--I really did--but it had to be done.

I left the apartment, leaving him on the ground bloody and covered in his own piss, and went to my car then drove off.

It was much later when I realized how much of a blunder this had been. It was inevitable that someone would see Ozzie and ask about the bruises. Word would spread. This took away my element of surprise. People would know that I was out, looking for information. This gave people the chance to stay away, avoid me. It also led Ozzie directly to the arms of the U.S. Attorney's Office.

Up to that point, he remained completely loyal. Even though he had been questioned repeatedly by the prosecutor, he was innocent as a lamb. A fact I wouldn't learn until much later.

Hindsight is a motherfucker.

I needed to be more cautious. I needed to take better steps. I wanted to avoid getting caught up by the cops anymore than I already had. There was a lot at stake, and a lot of individuals were invested in me. Many of them, however, would also be happy to watch me crash and burn.

I fucked up with Ozzie. I couldn't do it again.

But despite that huge fuck up, my mind kept returning to my silent partner. Bull was always very closed-mouthed, but I knew he was out there, somewhere, lurking in the shadows. He may not like the blunder I just made, but I knew he wouldn't judge me for it. We made a lot of money together, much of it because of my smarts, so he knew that I wasn't making stupid decisions.

When it came to business, Bull was always inconspicuous. When it was time to party, he became the Tasmanian Devil, loud, noticeable, boisterous, and a real braggart. When drunk, he'd spend money like it was going out of style, and had a good time socializing and womanizing.

I hoped everything was all right for Bull. I hoped he wasn't dealing with the same troubles I had. I hoped that we would find each other again, down the road, free, able to look back on all of this and laugh.

The universe had other plans for us, though.

The next time I would see him would be in a holding cell in a federal courthouse, surrounded by a cadre of U.S. Marshals. The courts, the government, and the media vilified us--treating us like we were terrorists.

I didn't know that was the future in store for us at the moment as I drove to Flatbush for another meeting, continuously hoping that I'd never see the inside of another cell.

I fucked up with Ozzie, but there was still a chance of making things right--not so much with him, but within the situation. It felt like a lost cause the more I thought about it, but I was never one to buy into that mentality.

Mind on autopilot, I shook out the thoughts of Ozzie, Bull, and my mistakes, and drove. This meeting was going to be tough, and I wanted to focus on that. Getting there was not a problem--I drove these streets hundreds of times before. It was what would happen at the meeting that had me concerned. The cat I was going to meet scared easily, which didn't boost my confidence as I was told he was scared to death of me.

He knew my reputation. Some of the fear he had was because of times when he'd seen me bring the pain to people who worked against my best interests. But he wasn't some punk. This was a guy who feared no one, a conflicting persona that made me unsure of what I was going to walk into.

As I reached my destination, my pager started exploding. The numbers coming up were familiar, but I didn't have the patience, or desire, to be questioned by anyone. From this, I knew that word about Ozzie had reached the streets.

While Ozzie ultimately kept his mouth shut with the feds, it seemed he had little problem letting everyone in the neighborhood know what had happened to him. It pissed me off. If

Ozzie was going to talk to any and everyone about me hitting him, causing my beeper to go off nonstop, then maybe he really couldn't be trusted. Perhaps he deserved to be hit.

No matter what, I had no energy to deal with the aftermath. I didn't care if people were panicking about how I reacted in the situation. None of that mattered. In my line of work, people were either friends or foes.

Or both.

21

———————

TRICKED

THINGS WERE RAPIDLY FALLING APART.

No matter how hard I tried to put things back into place, it seemed as if the universe was aligned against me.I was supposed to see it coming. I mentally prepared myself for any and all eventualities, but it all meant nothing when the scenario played out in real time.

It all came down to the gun that went missing during my arrest in New York. NYPD had obtained it from my car and sent it to forensics. From there, they traced the gun's purchase to Southern Gun World, a gun shop in Richmond, Virginia. They were hoping the forensic analysis of the gun would link it to any of the crimes associated with one, or more, of my forty-two indictments.

Forty-two indictments.

Can you believe that shit? Because I damn sure couldn't.

That gun alone gave me eight different federal gun violations, but none that the cops were after. The specific crime I allegedly perpetrated got added due to a set of fabricated evidence. I discovered this when reading documents I received before the trial.

The real reason they didn't charge me for the weapon when I was arrested in New York, was because they didn't want to act prematurely by doing something that could hinder their investigation. To be charged with 18 USC 1959, Violent Crimes in Aid of Racketeering, I didn't need to be the trigger man. Being in the vicinity of the crime, or knowing about it, is enough to land someone a life sentence.

I stopped worrying about the investigation and focused on securing myself more money. It was still coming in, but on a limited basis. I spooked a lot of people once loyal to me by confronting Ozzie, and ended up doing work I'd normally have Demus do. I came from the streets though, so getting my hands dirty was nothing new. I was back in the field, something I hadn't done in years. It actually felt good, moving around in the streets again, but it was admittedly a lonely existence.

I couldn't trust anyone.

I knew I was being watched.

People wanted me dead, and I was running out of time.

In this world, when you are in the streets, there are two types of graves that never run out of space. The cemetery and prisons. I wasn't trying to be a resident of either one.

My pager kept buzzing.

I paid it no mind, desiring a spliff to ease my mind, but I needed to salvage what I could and put things back in their proper place. Maybe, just maybe, I could remove all hazards and replace them with a better functional system, then things could play out as I expected. As I wanted. The problem was, I didn't have enough time, or people in my life, to start a new crew, nor did I intend to. I just needed the chance to influence an opportunity without allowing it to take shape on its own.

I had to get back down to Virginia.

I had to get there fast.

While driving through East Orange, I thought about the many mistakes I made in the past year. Some were due to miscalculations. Others were unavoidable consequences. But in this game, there was no room for mistakes. Every error will cost you something.

I yawned. "Damn."

My mind was fuzzy from my refusal to sleep. Reaching my New Jersey apartment, I checked the area thoroughly before going inside to get some shut eye. After 3 hours of rest, I was ready for the drive on I-95 down to Richmond.

I arrived on a Saturday evening, around 6:30 PM. I went straight to the house of a business associate. They informed me on everything that transpired during my absence.

There were a couple new players in town selling weight. Already, others were rushing in to fill my vacancy, but I knew these new players would experience a lot of difficulties--including violence--as they began their enterprise. Richmond guys disliked out-ot-towners coming into their city, hustling, fucking their women. Especially New Yorkers.

After leaving my business associate's, I went to my house. When circling the block, I noticed some new cars around the complex I hadn't seen before. Thinking nothing of it, I parked, went through the house's back door, and settled in for the night. Unaware that a car light flickered on in one of the vehicle's the second I was inside.

SEPTEMBER 8TH, 1995

I woke up early in the morning and got ready for the day, putting on a cashmere Pelle Pelle jacket, a pair of Clarks, a Jesus piece Cuban link chain, and some diamond rings. Once dressed, I rolled up a big spliff and looked around, admiring my comfortable little house, not knowing it would be the last time I'd have the chance to.

After rolling, I got up and exited using the back door again. While driving down to one of my partner's, I decided that I was done with Richmond. It was time to cut all ties, starting today.

I pulled up in front of Match Point apartments. Waited. Getting impatient, I blew the horn.

Mu hurried out with a cat I knew from Jersey named Ali-Rahm, a vicious craven who aspired to be top dawg. He had the survival instincts of a rodent, willing to do anything to get out of a jam, but I wouldn't find out about that until later, to my own detriment.

They both hopped in the passenger side, with Mu up front and Ali directly behind him.

"Fyngaz, what's the science?" Mu said.

"Man, I'm trying to leave this shit behind us," I said. "Need to cut our losses."

"You for real?"

"I think we've overstayed our welcome. The place is heating up."

Ali remained quiet, but his opinion did matter. I brought him down from Jersey to hustle with me, and he was very good at making money, even though he lacked the balls. Still, he made enough profit to venture on his own, and was capable enough to earn my trust.

We drove off to the projects in Richmond. I was on Hull St., at an intersection waiting for a green light, when a patrol car pulled up behind me. They turned their siren on.

Thinking they needed to pass me, I turned to move out their way.

They swerved with me.

I was about to be pulled over. I didn't panic, though. I owned the car, it was insured, I had my license, and I was clean.

As I pulled over, I noticed my two passengers pull out their guns simultaneously.

On cue, a voice on the police speaker boomed. "Jimmy Fingers, we know you are in there. Turn the car off, take the key out the ignition, throw them out the window and place both hands out the driver's window."

All hell broke loose.

Cars on both sides of the intersection made sudden U-turns, jumped the curb, and surrounded my car. Cops jumped out fully geared up, carrying assault rifles and pistols, each wearing blue jackets representing all sorts of agencies--FBI, ATF, DEA, and state troopers.

The speaker blared again. "Don't move, Jimmy Fingers. We have your head in our scopes."

I spotted a red dot aiming at my head in the rearview

mirror. I was completely surrounded and under the threat of violence.

"Fuck this, Fyngaz," Mu said, "we going all out. Ram those cars and let's go."

"Are you fucking crazy?" I snapped. "They don't have shit on me, and there's a beam on my head, you silly muthafucka."

I stepped out of the car before either could make the situation worse.

Two officers rushed over and forced me against a black SUV, while others secured my car with the passengers inside. An FBI agent came towards me and said, "Let me see your hands."

I showed him my right hand. "For what?"

"And the other."

I showed him the left.

His eyes went wide with excitement as he spoke into his walkie-talkie. "Suspect identified, we have Jimmy Fingers."

He cuffed me. Threw a hood over my head. Pushed me into the back of the SUV. We sped off. Through its tinted window, I saw Mu and Ali getting detained on the sidewalk as I was taken to joint task force headquarters.

Once processed, I was taken to Richmond city jail and placed in a cell, only to be moved two days later to a more secure facility in Orange County, Virginia, where I was locked up for 23 hours a day. A week later, a lawyer visited and introduced himself as my representative for the federal charges of possession of a weapon as a convicted felon and maintaining a stash house. All of these charges stemmed from my initial arrest when the FBI found 2 guns stuffed under the front passenger seat. Since the car was in my name, the guns were in my possession.

I sat in silence as my lawyer explained the details, stating how, "The stash house came from a raid on an apartment they said belonged to you, where they found large quantities of cocaine and cocaine base."

I went back to my cell, knowing I'd be facing some time, but still unaware of the grim reality created by a sealed indictment--with much more serious charges--that awaited me.

I spent my entire pretrial detention in the hole. When time came for the actual trial, I was placed in a 50,000 voltage black box restraint tied around my waist that the US Marshall held a switch for, ready to be pressed in the event I caused any issues. Two months later, after a lengthy and exhausting trial, I was found guilty of all charges--except one--of a 36 count superseding indictment. I was convinced my two lawyers sold me out. As sentencing was scheduled for three weeks in advance, I was already plotting on how I could liberate myself.

BOOK TWO COMING SOON

THE BID

This story provides an in depth look at a young black man's odds of freedom, by following the protagonist's quest to become something better while faced with innumerable obstacles, violence, tragedy, pain, religion, relationships, and loss when surviving within the BOP's vicious USP Penitentiaries as he goes up against courts, and a corrupt system, that lack empathy for any person of color.